END OF DARKNESS

Survive the Darkness Book 12

RYAN CASEY

GET A POST APOCALYPTIC NOVEL FOR FREE

To instantly receive an exclusive post apocalyptic novel totally free, sign up for Ryan Casey's author newsletter at: ryancasey books.com/fanclub

CHAPTER ONE

Tristan stood in the middle of the street and saw the death all around him.

The sky was a hellish shade of red. It was like the Devil himself had risen from below to watch the chaos unfold. The air was warm and humid. Specks of rain trickled down from those thick storm clouds above. Usually, when Tristan looked up into the sky, he could distance himself from his actions. From the horrors around him. From the sounds and the smells and the tastes. He could fool himself. Tell himself he was somewhere better.

That he was some*one* better.

But today felt different.

He stood and stared up at the sky, and he listened to the screams all around him. The desperate cries of mothers grieving for their fallen sons. The sound of children crying for their parents. Begging. Terrified.

And then the sound of more bullets.

Bullets cracking through the air.

The screaming getting louder.

The crying growing more desperate.

And then...

The screams fading away.

One by one, as more of these people fell.

One by one, until... silence.

A silence that was somehow even more horrifying than the screams.

Because of what that silence meant.

Death.

He looked up into those clouds, and he thought about Mum. He hadn't thought about Mum for a long time. Thinking about Mum wasn't usually such a good idea. Not because he didn't like her. He loved Mum very much.

But because thinking of Mum brought a moral dilemma crashing home.

Thinking of what Mum would say if she knew what he was doing.

If she knew the horrors he was responsible for.

He thought of her wide, brown eyes. Tears on her tanned face as she sat there on the balcony of her Spanish apartment.

He pictured her shaking her head.

Pictured her turning her back on him as he tried to explain everything to her.

"It's for the best, Mum. It's for..."

And then she was gone.

She was gone, and he was alone again.

"Tristan?"

He heard a voice somewhere ahead. Snapped right back into the moment.

Looked ahead and saw Amelia standing opposite him. Rifle in hand. Squinting.

"You with us?" she asked.

Tristan looked around. He saw the bodies lying on the side of the road. The twisted limbs and the bright red blood, so bright it looked fake.

He saw the vacant expressions on the faces of the dead.

Fathers stretching out their hands to try and reach their children, who lay dead just metres away from them.

He smelled those awful smells of death. Sweat. Piss. Shit. Blood.

And he tasted vomit.

His head spun.

His legs started shaking.

Growing weak.

He leaned forward, and he vomited onto the road beneath him.

"Hey," Amelia said, walking over to him. "You okay?"

Tristan stood there, staring down at the vomit on the road. He looked down into it, tasted the burning acid at the back of his throat.

And in his chest, he felt a crippling anxiety.

Heart racing.

Stomach churning.

Like he was being shaken.

Like something inside him had broken, and he was finally, *finally* seeing the reality of his crimes.

The horror of his actions.

Amelia put a hand on his back. Patted him. "It's okay. I know it gets too much sometimes. We all do. But just remember. It's for the best. These people, they're not the future. They're warmongers. They're rapists. They're... they're nasty little bastards, and you know they aren't the future of this country. We are. Right? We are."

He heard these words like he'd heard them so many times before. Usually, hearing them was enough to trigger him back into loyalty.

Because he was the future.

His people were the future.

Only... this time, he found he didn't believe those words as much.

This time, he found himself doubting them.

This time, he found himself asking a question that had been haunting him for a few days now.

A question he'd managed to suppress and resist for weeks.

Months.

Years.

A simple question.

But a question that threatened to change everything.

What if we're wrong?

He heard that question swinging around his mind like a battering ram, bashing against the insides of his skull.

And mixed with the sounds and the smells of death and the taste of vomit... he could feel himself slowly but surely spiralling out of control.

What if we're wrong about everything?

"You know what the General would say," Amelia said. "If we didn't have moments of weakness, we wouldn't be human."

He thought about the General, and his body went cold.

He thought about those steely blue, almost grey, eyes.

That short grey hair and the little bald patch in the middle of his head.

That smile.

That ever-present smile.

He thought about him, and instead of feeling the confidence and the devotion he usually felt... he felt something different entirely.

He felt repulsion.

He felt fear.

"Come on," Amelia said. "Pull yourself together. The General will be here soon. See."

Tristan turned around to the entrance of the community they called Eastbrook, and he saw them on the horizon.

Figures.

Hundreds of them.

More of his people, walking down that hill, towards this community, towards the smoke, towards the death.

And leading those people...

The General.

He stood there, shaking, wobbly on his feet. He tasted that vomit growing stronger. He felt the warm rain peppering down from above. Saw the bodies twitching at the side of the road. The signs of death and slaughter, all around him.

What if this isn't the right way forward?

He watched those figures grow closer and closer, down the slope, from the woods beyond, and he took a deep breath and forced those thoughts of resistance away.

Because he was in too deep now.

He was in far too deep to change anything anyway.

"I'm with you," Tristan said, standing tall, swallowing a lump in his throat.

"Good," Amelia said, slapping him on the back. "That's the Tristan I know. Anyway. We'd better get ready for his arrival. I think he'll be impressed with how quickly we swept through this place."

Tristan stood and watched as the figures approached.

As *he* approached.

And then he turned his gaze towards the police station.

Towards the place he'd let that man go.

The man called Billy.

He thought about Billy, and he thought about how close he'd been to killing the pair of them, and a small part of him wished he had. Wished he'd just put him out of his misery and ended it.

But a bigger part of him spoke up.

A bigger part of him hoped he'd seen something genuine in Billy.

A strength he couldn't quite put his finger on.

And a sense of leadership about him that could topple him and his people.

Strength and leadership that he *wanted* to topple his people.

He looked over at that police station, and as much as he knew his wishes were far-fetched... he couldn't help but pray.

And then he took a deep breath of the smoky air.

Turned around.

Stood tall and faced the oncoming figures.

Faced the General.

He had done a good job today.

They'd *all* done a good job today.

And there could be no other way.

It was all for the good of humanity.

It was for the good of the future.

It was for the survival of the nation—and the world.

He kept on telling himself these things as he stood there and waited for the arrival of the General.

But he couldn't shake that voice in his head that was growing louder and louder by the second.

What if this isn't the way?

CHAPTER TWO

"Y ou ready to do this?"

"Not entirely."

"Me neither."

"Hardly fills you with optimism, does it?"

Billy stood at the police station door and looked out at the hellscape he'd called home for years.

The sky was red. The streets were filled with bodies, lying flat, like they were part of the scenery.

And the worst thing about those bodies?

Some of them were twitching.

Some of them were trying to move, even though their legs had been blown off.

Some of them were crying, gargling blood.

It was all completely fucked up.

He could hear gunshots cracking and echoing somewhere in the distance. It sounded like a war zone. There were lots of gunshots earlier. Lots of explosions. The smell of smoke hung in the air, catching with every breath, making Billy cough.

But more than anything, his focus was on that crowd on the hill.

That oncoming crowd of Liberators getting closer and closer to his community.

To his home.

And as much as he wanted to stand up for his community—as much as he wanted to fight for his people and get the revenge he deserved—right now, his goals were immediate.

He needed to get home.

He needed to get to Rex.

He needed to rescue him.

And then he needed to get out of here—with as many survivors as he could.

If there *were* any survivors at all.

He remembered the promise he'd made to Steve as he lay dying in that cell. The shock of losing Steve still hadn't hit him properly. Not yet. And in a way, he had to bury that grief for a while.

He couldn't afford to grieve right now.

He couldn't afford any kind of self-reflection or introspection or any of that bullshit right now.

This was about action.

Pure action.

And he couldn't afford to stand around and wait much longer.

He looked at Marco, standing by his side. An unexpected ally, that was for sure. He didn't like the guy. He'd been a dick to him for years. But then, at the end of the day, when your community came under attack, you were all united in a way, weren't you?

And besides. Learning the truth about Marco's past, it all made a lot more sense.

He was a survivor, just like Billy.

Not just a survivor of the apocalypse. Not just someone who had learned to survive in a world devastated by the loss of power.

He was a survivor of abuse.

And for that reason, they were united.

"You sure we can make it?" Marco asked.

"No. No, I'm not. Are you?"

"Absolutely *fucking* not. But what other choice do we have?"

"Exactly," Billy said, turning around, back to the empty square outside the police station doors. "It's one step at a time now. One milestone at a time. Get to my place with our heads still on our shoulders. Get Rex. And then... well. We figure out where we go from there. 'Cause the speed those Liberators are approaching, I don't think we've got long to mess around."

Marco nodded. "I hear you."

Billy looked beyond the doors of the police station, out onto that square.

Empty.

For now, anyway.

They had to be ready to get out there.

They had to be ready to run to Billy's place.

They had to go.

He looked back around. Back at the corridor towards the cells. A lump swelled in his throat.

"I'm sorry for leaving you, Steve," he whispered. "But I'll do you proud. I'll fight for this community."

He turned around.

Took a deep breath.

And he stepped out of the temporary safety of those police station doors and into the open.

A mixture of emotions hit him, stepping out. A sense of freedom because he'd been cooped up in that cell for a long time.

But also fear.

Fear.

He felt exposed.

And seeing the sorry state Eastbrook was in—seeing that he hadn't had a chance to help stop this, or that nobody had listened to him when he'd *tried* to help... Yeah, a real fucking mixture of emotions about everything right now.

But again. This wasn't the moment for introspection.

Not anymore.

This was a moment for attempting to survive.

Somehow.

"We run down the alley between the old chemist and the post office," Billy said. "Then we see what the front of my street is like from there. There's the old tunnel too if we have to. The underpass. But... yeah. We've got to figure it out as we go."

Marco nodded. Kept on looking over his shoulder from left to right. Billy got it. It really did feel like someone was watching them. That it was just a matter of time before they were shot dead. Before they were just bodies on the street like everyone else.

There was nothing special about Marco.

There was nothing special about him.

But while they were alive, they had to do everything they could to try and get out of this place.

"You with me?" Billy said.

"I figure I don't have much choice."

"That'll do," Billy said. "Come on, then. Let's get across the street. Those Liberators are approaching far too quickly for my liking. And I'd really rather be away from here with as many of our people as possible before they get here."

Marco nodded.

Billy ran.

They didn't have far to go.

Across the square, towards the alleyway, and hopefully towards home.

Where *hopefully*, he'd find Rex waiting for him.

He just started running when suddenly he saw something in the corner of his eye that stopped him dead in his tracks.

Liberators.

Appearing out of nowhere on the street they were on.

Looking right at him and Marco.

CHAPTER THREE

Okay, so if there's one thing Billy *really* didn't want to deal with right now, it was a group of Liberators staring right at him and Marco.

He stood in the middle of the street. Heart racing fast. He felt frozen. Which was less than ideal, because if there's one thing he *really* didn't need to be right now, it was frozen to the spot.

The Liberators emerged from around the street corner. Four of them. All dressed in grey. All holding rifles in hand.

Looking right at Billy.

Right at Marco.

Walking right towards them.

Billy stood there. Heart racing. Chest tight. Why couldn't things be easy? Or, well, not *easy*, but even just more straightforward than it always seemed to be.

He'd only just made it out of the cells and barely had time to process Steve's—*Dad's*—death at all, and now here he was. Standing in the middle of the street and facing almost certain obliteration at the hands of these monsters.

"Well?" Marco said.

Billy looked at the Liberators, who approached. He wasn't

even sure they'd seen him because they didn't have their rifles raised. But then... they *must've* seen him, right? They were looking right at him. Right at Marco. Walking right towards them.

He stood there, and he realised he had no choice.

His and Marco's goal was the same. It hadn't changed.

They had to get down the alleyway between the old chemist and post office.

They had to get back to Billy's place.

They had to get to Rex and get him out of here, and...

He turned back to the Liberators, and his stomach sank.

They had their rifles raised.

Pointed right at him and Marco.

"Fuck," Billy said. "There's no more time to—"

Just as soon as he'd spoken, a cascade of bullets exploded from the rifles, right towards him and Marco.

He ran. Didn't think. *Couldn't* think. Just ran as fast as he could.

Towards the alleyway.

Towards his house.

Towards Rex.

He ran across the street. Past the dead bodies lying there, staring up blankly. He saw men. Women. Children. Didn't matter. Not to the Liberators. They were all fair game.

All lying in pools of their own blood.

Gunshot wounds on their foreheads, and their backs, and their chests.

He heard more gunshots. Saw bullets whizz past, felt them whoosh so close to his ankles.

But he kept his pained fists tight.

Kept on focusing on the alleyway.

He just had to get there, and then he was in the clear —for now.

Both were in the clear—for now.

He ran towards that alleyway opening when he saw something that made his stomach sink.

Two more of them.

Running down the alleyway.

Rifles raised.

Blocking their path.

"Shit," Billy said.

He didn't have time to turn around. Didn't have time to reassess. Didn't have time to think.

He had to make a spontaneous, reactive decision, and he had to live by it.

Or die by it.

More likely die by it.

He turned to the chemist beside the alleyway, and he grabbed Marco's arm. "In here."

He yanked Marco out of the line of fire just in time.

He bashed his way through the door to the old chemists—which was no longer anything because the door never locked. Definitely not safe or secure enough to hold any medical supplies.

He dragged Marco inside, around the empty shelves, towards the counter, towards the door at the back.

They could get through there.

They could get into the back, and they could escape out the back yard, and they could get out of this.

They could still get out of this.

He raced towards that door at the back of the chemists behind the counter.

Heard the Liberators getting closer.

Heard them closing in.

"Come on," he muttered. "Come on."

He slammed against that door.

Grabbed the handle.

Went to turn it.

His stomach sank.

No. Please, God, no.

"Billy?" Marco said. "What the fuck is it?"

Billy looked up at Marco. Looked into his wide, terrified eyes.

"It's... it's locked," he said.

"Locked? But there must be a key around here. Right?"

Billy nodded. He'd been in here before when he was helping clear out a spider infestation, something that really freaked out Caroline, one of the more melodramatic of the Eastbrook residents.

He remembered promising her he'd lock the door so no spiders could get out. But the key... where had he put the key?

The counter somewhere?

There had to be a key somewhere around the counter.

He lunged for the cupboard behind the counter when suddenly he froze in his tracks.

The shadows at the door.

The footsteps creeping inside.

The Liberators were here.

CHAPTER FOUR

Billy stood at the counter and watched the shadows of the Liberators emerge.

He crouched down in an instant, dragging Marco down with him. Hid behind the counter. He didn't want to have to hide right now. Didn't want to have to make such a cowardly move. He wanted to stand up to these people—these people who had destroyed his home. Murdered so many of his people. Murdered his father.

But at the same time, he knew he had to survive right now. Survival was a priority.

For Rex.

And for everyone else.

He crouched right there behind the counter and listened to the footsteps of the Liberators creak inside.

He listened to them get closer. Listened to them stepping around the chemists, step by step. They'd be on them in a matter of seconds. They didn't have time to think. Didn't have time to do *anything* other than act.

Hiding here for now had bought Billy and Marco a little more time.

But he couldn't hide here forever.

He listened to those footsteps get closer. It sounded like they were coming around both sides of the store, searching every inch of the place. So it wasn't even like he could make a distraction then make a break for it—he'd find himself running into trouble no matter which way he went.

He crouched there, heart racing faster, hands getting sweatier, and he looked back at the door. The key. If he could just search the drawers and find the key, then maybe he had a chance. A chance of getting out of here. A chance of escaping.

But he didn't have time to search any drawers.

He didn't have time to do anything.

He sat here behind the counter waiting for fate to step in, waiting for a miracle, when suddenly he saw something on the floor, right underneath the counter.

The key.

The key to the back door.

He remembered now. Sticking it under there, so it was close to the door. Close enough to unlock it if the time came that he needed to but hidden well enough that the supplies weren't so easy to access.

He saw it sitting there on the thin-carpeted floor.

Saw cobwebs underneath.

Spiders underneath.

And shadows, too.

Shadows of those feet moving his way.

He knew he didn't have time to think. Time to deliberate.

He had no time at all.

He reached under the cabinet.

Felt the soft tickle of cobwebs against his fingertips.

Felt little creepy crawlies dashing across the back of his hand and up his arm.

He stretched and grabbed the key, and then he pulled it out from under that cabinet.

"Now or never," Billy said.

He listened to those footsteps, and he knew he didn't have any time.

They were close.

So close.

He was going to get a bullet in the back.

He was going to get shot the second he stuck the key in the lock.

But what other choice did he have?

Sit here?

Wait for the inevitable?

Or take a gamble on something that *might,* just *might* get him out of this mess?

He gritted his teeth, and he thought of Steve, Aoife, Mum, and all those people he'd lost.

And he prepared to join them. He felt ashamed. Ashamed for letting them down. Ashamed for letting *Steve* down.

He closed his eyes, took a breath, and then he went to stand.

He lunged towards the door.

Buried the key into the lock with his shaking hand.

Turned it.

Then he lowered the handle.

Somehow still standing.

Somehow, no bullets in his back.

Somehow... still alive.

He didn't want to look back. Didn't want to go tempting fate.

He had to get out of here.

Just had to get away.

But then there was Marco, too.

He turned around to grab Marco when he saw something.

The Liberators.

They were standing with their rifles pointed right at him.

Right at Marco.

But they weren't firing.

They were just standing there, and they weren't firing.

Billy looked at them. It gave him the creeps. Because he'd seen them firing at everyone. He'd seen them slaughtering everyone indiscriminately.

And yet...

They were holding their fire around him.

They weren't shooting.

"Come on," Billy shouted, urging Marco to join him. "We need... we need to go. Now!"

Marco stood up, and they went to pull their triggers.

Billy grabbed him.

Dragged him through the door.

Slammed the door shut.

Stuck the key in the lock and turned it.

And then he ran with Marco by his side, over to the fence at the back of the chemists.

Hopped onto the bin and clambered over the fence.

Landed in the street and saw the row of terraced houses in the street opposite.

A street filled with more bodies.

His street.

He saw his house, and his stomach sank.

His front door was open.

He stood there, shaking with adrenaline. Listened to the Liberators behind, still banging away on the chemist door.

And as he stood there and waited to make his move across the street, somehow still alive, he couldn't help thinking about the way they'd held those rifles.

The way they'd pointed at him.

But the way they'd held fire.

He didn't know what it meant.

But right now, there was only one option.

"Come on," Billy said. "Let's... let's go to my place. Let's go save Rex."

Behind, he heard those Liberators banging on the door, and he couldn't stop thinking about how they'd held their fire...

CHAPTER FIVE

Billy looked across at his house and felt crippling anxiety deep in his stomach.

The sky was still this weird shade of red. Red sky at night, shepherd's delight, Mum used to say, back in the day. Meant it was going to be a nice day tomorrow, apparently. Red sky in the morning, fisherman's warning. Opposite effect.

Red sky in the afternoon? What the fuck did that mean?

They probably didn't make a rhyme for that because it was probably such a rare occurrence.

And yet... here they were.

In Hell itself.

He saw more bodies littered across the middle of the road. No Liberators in sight. But the group descending the hill was getting closer. They'd be in Eastbrook soon. They'd be here in no time.

And then...

Well. What then?

He thought back to the incident in the chemists just now.

The Liberators standing there.

Pointing their rifles at him.

But not firing.

Why weren't they firing?

And then, the second Marco reared his head... they opened fire.

Missed. Somehow. Thankfully.

But opened fire all the same.

What did it mean?

What did any of it mean?

Fuck. He'd have time to think about all that, eventually. He'd have time to go through and process everything. And he had a hell of a lot to process, that was for sure.

But right now, it was still a case of taking things step by step.

Survival was still the priority.

He closed his burning eyes and took a deep breath of the smoky air.

"Come on," Billy said. "The sooner we get this done with, the better."

He crept across the street. He didn't want to look left or right 'cause he really didn't want to see any Liberators right now. He'd rather just bury his head in the sand and not know at this point, to be honest. He'd cheated death far too many times. Far, *far* too many times.

He figured he didn't have many more lives left. Many more chances left.

He tried not to look at the bodies on the road, but that was pretty much impossible. A man called Rupert, lying face flat in his own blood. Skull cracked, brains spilling out.

A woman called Giselle, hole in her neck and her back, skin totally pale, and a look of horror in her bright blue eyes.

He shook his head, and he looked away. He felt so useless seeing them all lying here. He'd tried to help. He'd tried to fucking help, and nobody had listened, and this was the reason the place had been destroyed.

But he couldn't focus on that. They were bound to be sceptical of him. The Liberators had torn the community in two and filled Eastbrook with paranoia.

He knew how things looked. He couldn't hold it against the people, or the leaders, of Eastbrook.

He couldn't even hold it against Marco.

He glanced up as he reached the pavement. Over to the left.

The streets were quiet.

Empty.

He looked over to the right, and he saw those Liberators making their way down the slope.

So close now.

They'd be here soon. Here in no time at all.

He didn't want to be anywhere near here when they got here.

He looked around at his front door and felt his stomach sink again.

The door was open.

He never left the door open.

Especially not with Rex inside. As old and lazy as Rex was, if he spotted an open door, he'd be out sniffing away, and the blind old bat would probably never get home again.

"He'll be here," Marco said.

Billy looked around at him. "Huh?"

"Rex," Marco said. Eyes focused ahead. "I know... I know how much he means to you. He'll be here. He's a home bird. Right?"

Billy looked back at the front door to his house, and he took a deep breath. "You know, that might actually be the nicest thing you've ever said to me."

"Don't get used to it."

Billy laughed. Marco smirked.

The pair of them stood there in this horrifying and absurd and completely nail-bitingly tense moment, and they braced themselves.

"You've got this," Marco said.

"Okay. Easy on the reassuring talk now."

"Too much?"

"Yeah. Probably. Still just processing this whole you and me getting along thing."

Marco nodded. "Duly noted."

Billy walked down the cracked, uneven pathway towards his house.

Past the tall grass, which Steve always used to insist needed cutting, even though Billy preferred the wild look.

Past the bees buzzing around the flowers, oblivious to the horrors going on around them.

And up to the door.

He stood at the open door.

Took another deep breath.

Looked around at Marco.

"You ready?" Marco asked.

Billy swallowed a lump in his throat, and he nodded. "Ready as I'll ever be."

And then, stomach twisting itself into knots, he stepped through the open door and into his home.

CHAPTER SIX

The second Billy stepped inside his home, he had a bad feeling he wouldn't find Rex.

Or worse than that. He had a bad feeling he would find Rex in a terrible, terrible state.

He looked around his lounge. A place he used to spend so much time. It felt like forever since he'd last sat in here, even if it was just a matter of days. So much had happened in such a short space of time. Everything had changed.

But at least his house was still standing.

At least he still had a chance.

He heard a couple more explosions of gunfire outside, and he came crashing right back down to earth. The smell of smoke in the air outside and burning, making its way inside.

This wasn't a moment for reflection.

This was a moment for action.

"Come on," Billy said. "No time to stand around."

"You can say that again," Marco said.

He walked through the lounge and into the kitchen. Still no sign of Rex in here. Which wasn't completely surprising. Only time he usually went down to the kitchen was when Billy put food out for him—and most of the time, he just gave him food in the bedroom now, anyway.

He stood at the bottom of the stairs and looked up into the darkness.

"Please, Rex," he whispered. "Please don't leave me too."

He walked up the stairs. Slowly at first. But then quicker. Time was of the essence. The Liberators were crawling around Eastbrook. He didn't have time to mess around.

He had to find Rex.

He couldn't leave this place without him.

As he reached the top step, he thought about his other goal. The goal of finding more survivors. Finding enough survivors not only to get out of this place but to stand with him when he fought back against the Liberators—when he fought back for the sake of his home.

He didn't know how he was going to do that. Especially since he hadn't seen any other survivors.

But fuck. He could figure that out when the time was right.

Eyes on the goal, Billy.

Eyes on the frigging goal.

He reached the top step and turned around to face his bedroom.

The door was closed.

All the doors were closed.

His stomach sank. Because he didn't think he'd left Rex closed in alone.

And then another thought crossed his mind.

Shit. What if he wasn't here after all?

He'd given Rex the free run of the house when he'd walked off into the night to ditch the knife, hadn't he?

Or had he kept him shut in the bedroom?

He couldn't remember. Everything was so frigging blurry.

He reached the bedroom door.

Stood in front of it.

Only one way to find out...

He turned the handle.

Pushed the door open.

And he held his breath as he looked inside.

He looked around.

Looked at the bed.

Looked at the wardrobes.

Looked at the little cushion where Rex spent the bulk of his life these days.

There was no wagging tail to greet him.

There was no slobbering tongue against his face.

And there was no snoring, either.

Rex was nowhere to be seen.

He stood there, heart racing. Rex was gone. He didn't know where he'd gone, but he wasn't here. And that didn't look good.

"I'm sorry," Marco said. "It's... it's like I said. I know how much that dog meant to you."

Billy stood there and swallowed a lump in his throat. It was impossible not to feel deflated upon not finding Rex.

But at the same time, another possibility entered his mind.

"Steve," Billy said.

"What?"

"If—if anything happened to me, Steve would've taken care of Rex. He wouldn't've just left him to die."

He walked out of his bedroom, past Marco, and towards the top of the staircase.

"You really suggesting we run down to Steve's right now? Time's running out."

"Time's *running* out," Billy said. "But it hasn't run out yet."

Marco shook his head. "I don't think I can do this."

"Then don't do this. I'm not leaving Rex behind. He's all I've..."

He stopped, then. Right at the top of the stairs. Marco was silent. Not saying a word. And Billy wanted to keep it that way.

"Billy—"

"Don't," Billy said.

"I just—"

"Don't. Okay? Don't."

Marco opened his mouth, went to say something again, then closed his lips, lowered his head, and sighed. "I'm with you. I'm not turning my back on you now. I've already fucked up enough as it is. I've... I've got your back."

Billy looked right into his eyes, and he nodded back at him. "Then there's no more time to waste. We've got to go."

He climbed down the stairs.

Rushed towards his front door, fully aware he was never coming back to this place he'd called home for so, so long.

He looked around. Remembered the happy times he'd had here. The settled times he'd had here.

The beers he'd drunk with Steve here and the laughs he'd had here.

He took a deep breath, nodded, and went to walk towards the front door.

And that's when he heard footsteps.

Creaking.

In the kitchen behind him.

They weren't alone in here.

Someone was here with them.

CHAPTER SEVEN

The second Billy heard the footsteps, he froze.

There was someone in here in the house.

In the kitchen.

Right *fucking* behind him.

He stared at the front door, right ahead. Listened to the gunfire outside. The screams. Smelled the smoke in the air. And thought about the footsteps of those Liberators getting closer, and closer, and closer...

He didn't want to turn around.

He didn't want to look back.

He didn't want to look death in the eye again.

But what fucking choice did he have?

He turned around. Saw Marco standing on the stairs behind him, frowning.

And then he saw the kitchen.

Nobody there.

No Liberator standing there, rifle raised.

Nobody at all.

"What's up?" Marco asked.

"Heard somebody."

"Huh?"

"In the kitchen," Billy said. "I heard somebody."

He walked slowly towards the kitchen. Part of him knew he should just walk away. Get the hell out of the front door while he had the chance. Those Liberators heading down the hill would be here in no time—if they weren't here already. He really couldn't afford to dick around.

But at the same time... he couldn't shake that curiosity.

Someone was in his home.

He needed to know who it was.

He walked over to the door at the back of the kitchen. Held his breath. Realised very suddenly just how vulnerable he was. He didn't have any guns. Any knives. He didn't have anything at all to protect himself with.

But fuck it. Again, he didn't have the luxury of time on his side.

"We should go, Billy," Marco said.

"I need to check this."

"We don't have much time."

"I'm well aware of that."

He held his breath.

Stopped. Right at the kitchen door.

And then he stepped inside.

The kitchen was just as empty as he'd left it.

Nobody in sight.

Only... he'd heard those footsteps. He'd heard them. He wasn't stupid.

He looked around. Studied every inch of the kitchen. Waiting for someone to jump out. To catch his eye.

But there was nobody here.

"Leave it, Billy," Marco said. "We've—we've really got to get out of here. Right this second. Okay?"

Billy nodded. And then he went to turn around and walk away.

Suddenly, he heard it.

Rustling.

Rustling over to the right.

He looked around, and his stomach sank.

The cupboard under the stairs.

There was somebody under there.

And there were patches of blood leading the way to the cupboard.

He swallowed a lump in his throat. Again, he knew he should just walk away. Knew he should get the hell out of this place.

But that noise.

That noise under the stairs.

What if it wasn't a Liberator?

What if it was a survivor?

What if it was Rex, somehow?

He walked across the kitchen, over towards the door.

"Billy," Marco gasped. "We—we really need to get the hell out of here. Seriously, mate."

But Billy didn't hear him.

Or rather, he didn't listen.

He kept on walking.

Following the patches of blood.

Over towards the door.

He stopped in front of it.

Felt his heart racing in his chest.

He waited. Waited and listened but didn't hear a thing. Not anymore.

He took a deep breath.

Grabbed the handle.

"Now or never," he muttered.

And then he opened the door to the cupboard under the stairs.

CHAPTER EIGHT

Billy was right. He wasn't alone.

But when he opened the door to the cupboard under the stairs, it wasn't who he expected to find.

"Sergeant Kirk?" Billy said.

Sergeant Kirk sat in the cupboard under Billy's stairs, staring right back up at him. His eyes were wide. His puffy face looked pale. He wasn't saying anything. Just staring up towards Billy and Marco. Fear in his eyes.

"What—what are you doing in..."

Billy stopped then.

Because he saw the blood on Sergeant Kirk's stomach.

He'd been shot. Blood spilled between his shaking fingers. There was a puddle of blood right underneath him, which his large body was sitting in.

He looked down at Sergeant Kirk, and he felt a combination of emotions. Frustration that this man had arrested him. Locked him and Marco away and not taken their warnings about the Liberators seriously.

But more than anything, Billy felt sympathy.

Total sympathy.

Because Sergeant Kirk was one of his people. He was a resident of Eastbrook.

And he was in a bad, bad way.

"We need to get you out of here," Billy said.

"Billy," Marco said.

Billy gritted his teeth, turned around to Marco. "What now?"

Marco stood there, shaking his head. Stared at Billy with wide eyes. "It's—it's too late. There's no time. And you know it."

Right on cue, Billy heard the shouts and the cries outside. The smell of smoke filled his nostrils. And the sense of urgency intensified inside once again.

They needed to get away from here.

The Liberators were close. The larger group on the hill was closing in.

They were running out of time.

"We can't leave him behind," Billy said.

He walked over to Sergeant Kirk's side and tried to lift his immense weight.

But on trying to lift him, Sergeant Kirk let out an enormous cry.

A cry so loud Billy was sure it'd alert the attention of anyone nearby.

Marco shook his head. "Billy, he's—he's shot. He's shot, and he can barely move. We can't save him."

"I won't give up on him," Billy said.

He went to lift him again, tried to drag him to his feet.

But again, Kirk let out an agonised cry.

Thick blood spluttered out from his stomach, down his legs, and onto that puddle on the floor.

"Please," Kirk begged. "Pl... please."

Hearing Kirk so desperate and weak was haunting. Because he was usually so composed. He was usually so strong.

But right now, all that strength and assertiveness had left him.

He was dying.

He was bleeding out.

And there was nothing Billy could do for him.

He stood there by Sergeant Kirk's side. Heard him spluttering. Heard him struggling. And he saw the look on Marco's face, too. The look of sadness in his eyes.

He'd given up on Kirk already.

He'd let go of Kirk already.

And maybe Billy needed to do the same.

But then he remembered his promise to Steve.

The promise to fight for this community.

To fight for these people and to never stop fighting.

He remembered the promise he'd made, and he knew he couldn't just give up.

"Get his right side," Billy said.

"What?"

"Get his right side, right now. I'll get his left."

"Billy—"

"It's not going to be easy. But we can get him out of here. We can go through the back. And we—and we can find supplies for him. Get him stitched up. He's going to be okay. You're going to be okay, Kirk."

But Marco just stood there. Staring at the cupboard under the stairs. Shaking his head.

"Marco!" Billy shouted. "Give me a hand, right this second."

He saw Marco open his mouth and look over his shoulder.

And then he saw him turn back around and reluctantly walk over to Billy. "You're going to get us both killed."

"I'd die for my people. For my community. Wouldn't you?"

"Yes. But I don't want to die for nothing."

Billy grabbed the underside of Kirk's arm again. Marco got the other side.

"This isn't going to be pleasant, Kirk. But you're going to be okay. We've got you, okay? We've got you, and we're going to get out of here. On three, Marco. Three, two—"

"Wait."

"What?"

"You said on three. And then you counted down from three."

"Really?" Billy said. "Community's about to be completely obliterated and *that's* what you're bothered about right now?"

"I'm just trying to make sure we get it right, that's all."

"Whatever. Whatever, okay? Counting down from three. Three. Two. One..."

Billy lifted.

Marco lifted.

And for a second, for just a solitary second, Billy felt himself holding on to Sergeant Kirk, and he felt a glimmer of hope.

And then something awful happened.

A scream.

A deafening scream from Kirk.

"Fuck. Billy. His—his belly."

Billy didn't understand what Marco was talking about.

Not until he looked down at Sergeant Kirk's wound.

Instead of just blood—and there was still *lots* of blood—he saw intestines spilling out.

The pressure of lifting him must've forced them out of the wound.

And now they were tumbling out of his body towards the flood below.

Marco let go of Kirk's right side.

Vomited all over the kitchen floor.

Billy tried to hold on to Kirk as he screamed, cried, and then collapsed on the floor beside him, where he fitted, bled out, clutching onto his guts.

He looked at this sorry scene before him. The smell of vomit and undigested food—both from Marco and from Kirk's innards. The taste of blood on his lips. And the feel of it crusting on his palms.

He watched Kirk shake, blood frothing from his lips, and then go still.

And he knew he'd failed.

He knew he'd failed again.

"We should've left him," Marco gasped. "We should've... we should've just left him..."

Billy looked down at Kirk's dead body, his final agonising moments fresh in his memory, and he heard Marco's words circling around his mind.

We should've left him...

He was about to tell Marco to pull himself together because they had to go when he heard something that filled him with horror.

The front door to his house.

Opening.

Liberators.

CHAPTER NINE

Billy heard the front door to his house open, and he knew he was in deep, deep shit.

He stood in the kitchen, right opposite the cupboard under the stairs. Marco stood beside him. Vomit trickling down his chin. A patch of sick on the floor, where he'd thrown up. It smelled bad. Really bad.

But not nearly half as bad as the smell from Kirk's disembowelled body under the stairs.

He heard the footsteps creeping through the lounge and towards the kitchen, and he was in absolutely no doubt about who it was. A Liberator. Absolutely no fucking doubt about it. 'Cause who else would it be?

They'd heard Kirk's dying screams. They'd come to investigate.

And now he and Marco were fucked.

Totally fucked.

He stood there, and he looked under the stairs at Kirk's body. At the innards in a bundle in his dead arms. It was like he'd just delivered a baby and was holding onto it proudly.

Snakelike intestines spilling out of his arms and onto the bloody patch on the floor beneath him.

"We've got to run," Marco said. His voice hoarse after throwing up.

Billy nodded. Marco was too fucking right about that.

He went to run towards the back door.

He had to hope he made it in time.

No more time to fuck about.

No more time to waste.

He had to...

He reached the kitchen window, and he saw them.

Two of them.

In his yard.

And walking towards the back door.

"Liberators," he said. "More of them. Shit."

He stood there, heart racing, frozen. Liberators in the house. Liberators were in the back yard. They were coming at him from both sides, and they were closing in. Time was running out.

"What're we gonna do now?" Marco asked. "What the hell are we gonna do now?"

Billy stood there and watched those Liberators close in from the back.

Listened to the footsteps in the lounge, getting closer to his kitchen.

He stood there, and as much as he knew he was cornered, and as fucked as he knew he was, there was only one thing he could do.

"Under the stairs," Billy said.

"What? But—"

"There's no other way," Billy said.

He dragged the door open again.

Saw Kirk staring up at him from the darkness.

Shook his head and looked away, the smell of death making him want to puke.

"Come on," Billy said. "It's our only chance."

Marco's mouth moved, but no words came out. He looked like he was pissed at Billy but didn't have the time to formulate any insults right now.

"Fuck," Marco gasped, staggering towards Billy, towards the cupboard under the stairs. "If I die in a cupboard under the stairs like I'm fucking Harry Potter or something, it's on you."

Billy saw the Liberators right by the back door.

He pulled the door to the cupboard under the stairs shut.

And then darkness surrounded him.

He sat there under the stairs. Felt the dampness from Kirk's blood seeping through his jeans. He could smell blood in the air, so strong and rusty. And he could smell sick, too. And a strong smell of off milk. He wanted to believe it was just Marco's sick. He didn't want to consider that it might be the smell of Kirk's innards.

He kept still as he heard the back door click open.

As he heard the footsteps enter the kitchen.

And he held his breath as he braced himself for whatever was about to happen.

He held still. Very still. Sat there in the darkness and waited.

And as he sat there, he couldn't shake the feeling that this was on him.

This was all on him.

He should've got away from here while he had the chance. They both should.

But then what was he supposed to do?

Just give up on Kirk?

Give up on his people?

No. He couldn't do that. That wasn't... well, *him*.

He'd done the right thing. And if he died, then he'd die knowing he'd tried fighting for his people.

He heard those footsteps get closer, and he knew time was running out. He looked around under here in the darkness.

Looked for something he could use as a weapon. Something he could fight with.

He looked around and prayed for a miracle.

But this time, he didn't think he was getting his miracle.

He sat there, and he watched the door as the footsteps got nearer.

He watched the doors, and he waited for the Liberators to open them up.

For them to open fire.

And then...

And then he remembered.

The way they'd stood in the chemists.

The way they'd pointed their rifles at him.

The way they'd spared him.

For some reason, they'd spared him.

Why?

Was he just lucky?

Or was there more to all this than he thought?

He waited for them to reach the door, and as he sat there, heart racing, he figured he really didn't want to risk finding out.

But he wasn't going to have a choice.

Not when they got here.

He closed his eyes.

Swallowed a sickly lump in his dry throat.

Took a deep breath, and he prayed.

For a second, a split second, he heard nothing.

No footsteps.

No movement.

Nothing.

And then, after that moment's silence, the doors to the cupboard under the stairs clicked open.

CHAPTER TEN

Billy heard the doors to the cupboard under the stairs creak open, and he knew the end was imminent.

He squeezed his eyes shut. There was nothing more to see. He knew what was coming. The sooner the Liberator got on with it and pulled the trigger, the better. He stared into the darkness and braced himself for a different kind of darkness to follow. An eternal darkness. An endless darkness.

The void to end all voids.

His heart raced, and he heard the blood whooshing through his skull. His body was frozen solid, unable to move a muscle. He could taste vomit and smell it, too.

Vomit and blood.

And as he sat there, back against the cupboard wall under his stairs—the place poor Sergeant Kirk had dragged himself to, of all places—he didn't feel proud of his efforts. He didn't feel satisfied that he was going to die fighting for his community.

He felt ashamed.

Ashamed he hadn't been able to do more.

Ashamed he hadn't gone about things better.

Ashamed at all the people who had died because of him.

And all the people who *were* going to die because of him.

He sat there, and he waited for the end, and all he could think of was Steve—Dad—and how sorry he was.

I'm sorry I couldn't save them.

I'm sorry I couldn't fight.

He held his eyes shut and waited for the bang.

But he didn't hear anything.

He didn't want to open his eyes. Didn't want to look.

But this was dragging out.

It was dragging out, and Billy needed to know why.

He opened his eyes just slightly, and he saw the Liberator standing there, pointing the rifle at Billy.

There was just one of them. One bloke that he could see.

Standing with the rifle pointed at him.

Dressed in grey.

And there was something... *odd* about how he looked at Billy.

Just like the Liberators in the chemists had looked at him, too.

Why weren't they firing?

Why was he different?

What was happening?

"What..." Billy started. "Why aren't you... why aren't you firing?"

The Liberator didn't say a word.

Just kept his rifle focused on Billy, whose heart raced so fast he was pretty sure it was going to just give up on him at any moment.

Billy looked up at the Liberator. Looked right into his steely grey eyes.

"Why aren't you firing? Why... why aren't you firing me?"

The Liberator lowered his rifle.

And then he turned to Marco, who sat beside Billy.

Lifted his rifle and went to squeeze the trigger.

Billy didn't even think.

He threw himself in front of Marco, blocking him from sight.

"Get out of the way," the Liberator said.

"No. Not until you tell me why you aren't firing at me."

"Get out of the way," the Liberator repeated. "I'm warning you. Move. Now."

He crouched in front of Marco, and he knew there was absolutely no way he was moving.

Because for whatever reason, these Liberators were sparing him.

And if that gave him the armour he needed, then he had to use it.

"Move," the Liberator said. "Right this second."

"Why the fuck would I move? Tell me what you want. Tell me why you're destroying our community. And tell me... tell me why you're not shooting me."

The Liberator stared back down at Billy, rifle still pointed at him.

And then he took a deep breath, and he sighed.

"Because we are following orders," he said.

"Orders? Orders from who?"

He looked away, this Liberator. Just for a second, he looked away. And when he looked back, Billy swore he saw a glimpse of fear in this man's wide eyes.

"Move out of the way, or I'll say you died in an accidental shooting."

"I think I'll take my chances."

"Really? Then that's on you."

He lifted the rifle.

Pointed it right at Billy's head.

And Billy waited for the click of the trigger.

He waited for the end.

He crouched right in front of Marco, and one thing that struck him?

At least he knew he was going to die protecting one of his people.

It wasn't much, but it was something.

He took a deep breath, and he braced himself for the sudden pain followed by oblivion.

Gritted his teeth.

Pressed right up to Marco's shaking body, tight against him.

"Do it," Billy spat. "Get it done with."

The Liberator held the rifle to his head.

And then he shook his head and looked down at the floor.

"I really didn't want to have to do this," he said.

And then he looked back up at Billy, right into his eyes.

Tightened his grip around the trigger.

And then Billy heard the bang.

CHAPTER ELEVEN

Billy heard the Liberator's rifle bang, and he knew his life was over.

But he was still conscious.

He was still aware of the darkness behind his closed eyes.

He could still feel Marco shaking beside him and hear the ringing in his ears from the explosion.

He could still smell vomit and shit and piss and blood.

And he could still feel the dampness from Kirk's blood pooling beneath him.

He sat there in confusion as his ears continued to ring, and he opened his eyes.

The Liberator lay flat on the floor right in front of him.

Blood pooled out of his neck and onto the kitchen floor below him. He'd landed right in Marco's sick, which was a fate Billy would wish on nobody.

He stared at the Liberator's body lying there.

At the rifle in his hands.

And he saw a window of opportunity opening before him. Because for whatever reason, the other Liberators approaching the house had moved on. They hadn't followed their friend into the kitchen—as far as Billy could tell, anyway.

He couldn't hear anybody at all.

He looked at Marco, who was rooted to the spot. Staring widely at the Liberator's dead body in front of him. He had no idea who'd done this. Who was responsible for this. How it'd happened. Or where that person was.

But one thing was for sure.

They had to get the hell out of here while they had the chance.

"Come on," Billy said. "We've... we've got to get out of here."

Marco didn't say a word. He just nodded.

Billy crawled out from the cupboard under the stairs. The kitchen was silent. Definitely nobody else in here.

And it didn't sound like there was anybody else in the house, either.

They were off the hook.

They had a chance to get out of here.

"Come on," Billy said, waving for Marco to follow him. "The longer we hang around here, the more chance one of those bastards'll catch up with us."

But Marco wasn't moving.

He was still just sitting there.

Staring ahead.

"Marco?"

Marco lifted his head.

Looked Billy right in the eyes.

And then, finally, he spoke.

"Thank you," he said.

Billy nodded. "It's... it's okay—"

"You risked your life for me. After... after everything that happened between us. You still risked your life for me. Thank you."

Billy half-smiled. Marco had a point. He'd been a dick to Billy all these years—and he might just have played a part in getting his community obliterated, seeing as he was the one who'd forced Billy out of Eastbrook in the first place.

But then...

If that'd never happened, then Billy wouldn't have run into Meg or the Liberators or found out about any of this impending destruction.

"In a weird way, we'd probably all be dead if it wasn't for you," Billy said. "Now come on. We can't waste any more time here."

Marco climbed out from under the stairs. The pair of them stood there in the kitchen, the body of the Liberator at their feet.

Billy looked at the rifle, then up at Marco.

"Mind if I do?" Billy asked.

Marco nodded. "Be my guest."

Billy grabbed the rifle from the Liberator's hands. Heavy. Seemed pretty high-tech stuff. The best quality gear Billy had seen for a long, long time.

He looked down at the dead Liberator, and he wondered what these people's motives were.

And he wondered why so many of them were sparing his life.

It didn't make sense. None of it made sense.

And again, Billy felt like he didn't even have time to ponder what the fuck was going on because it'd been breakneck ever since Steve died...

Shit.

Steve was dead.

It was so recent that it still hadn't sunk in.

He looked up out the back window. Out into his yard. He didn't know where the other Liberators had gone. But he knew they weren't in here right now. Which meant he had a chance.

A chance he had to take.

"Let's get out of here," Billy said.

Marco nodded, followed him out through the kitchen door and back outside.

The humid afternoon air was such a relief to Billy. One of those luxuries he never thought he'd experience again. He could smell smoke. But there were no sounds of screaming anymore. There were no gunshots.

There was just silence now.

And it was creepy as fuck.

He looked across his yard, over to the back gate, and he knew what he had to do.

He had to go out there.

He had to walk down the alleyway at the back of the yards.

He had to go to Steve's, and he had to get Rex.

And then he had to get the hell out of here.

With Marco, and... well. Whoever else was still alive.

Although he was losing hope on that front.

He looked back at the kitchen. Towards that dead Liberator. Someone had helped them. Helped them, then done a runner.

He didn't know who it was. But it proved he still had allies around, even if he didn't know exactly where that help was coming from.

He walked towards the alleyway. Poked his head out. Checked left. Checked right. Rifle tight in his grip.

Nobody in sight.

A chance to get away.

"All clear," Billy said.

And then they ran. The pair of them ran down the alleyway towards Steve's place, not speaking, not doing anything that could hold them up.

Just hoping.

Hoping for a fucking miracle.

The closer Steve's got, the more nervous Billy grew.

What if Rex wasn't here?

Or what if he was dead already?

How was he going to say goodbye to someone else?

And then more questions gnawed at him.

Who had saved him?

Why were the Liberators not firing at him?

What the fuck did they *really* want?

He reached the gate at the back of Steve's house.

Stopped, right beside, and looked at Marco.

Marco raised his eyebrows.

"You ready?" he asked.

Billy nodded. "I've got to be."

He pushed the gate open, and he saw something right away that filled him with fear.

Rex.

Lying right there.

Right in the middle of the yard.

Totally still.

CHAPTER TWELVE

Billy saw Rex lying there in the middle of Steve's yard, totally still, and he felt his entire world crumbling.

But then Rex lifted his head.

He turned around, looked at Billy, and wagged that docked little tail of his.

Elation and relief filled Billy's body. A smile stretched across his face. "Rex," Billy gasped, running towards him.

"Watch out, Billy," Marco said. "We don't know if there's any of those Liberators close."

But Billy didn't hear him.

Nothing else mattered anymore.

All that mattered was Rex.

He fell to his knees and let Rex lick his face with his big, slobbery tongue. He felt tears welling up, his throat wobbling.

"I'm sorry for leaving you, old boy. I'll never leave you again."

He held on to Rex's big, warm body. He'd never felt this happy in his entire frigging life. From devastation to relief, all in a moment.

He was okay.

He was alive.

He was right here.

"Billy," Marco said.

Billy moved back a little. Rex sat there, panting away, tongue dangling out.

As much as Billy wanted this moment to last forever, he knew he couldn't hang around here much longer.

He had to get away.

"Come on, Rex. Let's... let's get out of here."

He ruffled Rex's fur, then he stood back up and walked over to Marco. Rex limped along without a care in the world. He was slower than he used to be, but he was walking, so that was something.

"Probably stuck around here long enough," Billy said.

"I've been telling you that for ages now," Marco said. "Out the back?"

"Think it's our best bet. Come on."

He ran over to Steve's back gate. And as Marco and Rex stepped out, he found himself looking back at Steve's place.

Looking at the little table at the top end of the garden where they should be enjoying a beer right now.

At the kitchen, where the pair of them would grab dinner and stay awake laughing about random shit til the early hours.

Tears clouded his vision.

A lump bobbed around his throat.

So many things he'd taken for granted.

So many things he missed already.

"Billy?" Marco said.

Billy turned around. "Yeah. I know. I..."

He saw something, then.

Something that made his stomach sink.

"Shit," he said.

Marco frowned. "What?"

Billy nodded down the alleyway behind the houses.

Marco turned and looked. "Oh. Fucking hell. These fuckers really never give up, do they?"

Liberators were running down the alleyway. They were a fair distance away. But he didn't want to stand around here much longer or give them a chance to catch up.

They might spare him for whatever weird reasons they had. But he couldn't be so confident the same thing would happen to Marco—or to Rex.

"We've got to go through Steve's," Billy said. "No other choice."

Marco nodded. "Too fucking right. Not too keen on sticking around here while they're—"

The sound of gunfire.

A bullet cracking into the wall right beside Marco.

"Shit," Marco gasped. "You absolutely sure these fuckers are still holding fire?"

"Only for me," Billy said.

He slammed the gate shut, and the pair of them and Rex ran across the yard.

"You know what would be funny right now?" Billy said. "And also really fucking typical?"

"Go on."

"If Steve locked his back door, and we couldn't get in."

"Don't even talk like that."

Billy reached the back door.

He tried to turn the handle.

And, of course, it didn't budge.

"Don't tell me. Just... just tell me it's unlocked."

"Okay," Billy said. "It's unlocked."

"Really?"

"No."

"Fuck. Why did you say it was unlocked?"

"Because you told me to tell you it was unlocked."

"Fucking hell," Marco said, shaking his head.

The pair of them stood there and listened to the footsteps of the Liberators get closer.

They stood there and listened as they approached the gate to Steve's yard.

And Billy looked down at the rifle in his hands.

"I guess there's only one option now," he said.

Marco nodded. "It seems that way."

Billy stood there.

Rifle raised.

Pointed.

Waiting for the Liberators to arrive.

Waiting for the perfect moment to pull the trigger.

He waited as those footsteps got closer.

As they slowed, right outside the gate.

Come on. Show your faces, you murderous fuckers.

And then something weird happened.

The Liberators just kept on running.

The footsteps got further away again.

Further and further away until eventually...

They were gone.

Billy stood there. Marco stood there. Rex stood there.

All of them totally still.

All of them—barring Rex, maybe—totally confused about what the fuck just happened or what was going on.

"They... they've gone?" Marco said, echoing Billy's thoughts.

Billy walked over to the gate again, Marco and Rex close behind.

He pulled it open, just a crack.

Then he bobbed his head out.

Scanned both sides.

"Yeah," he said. "They... they're gone. Come on."

He stepped out of the yard with Marco and Rex. Walked towards the turn at the end of the alleyway, which would take them out onto the road. He didn't like this. Something didn't feel right about it. One bit.

"I can't believe they'd just walk past us," Marco said. "It just… It doesn't make sense."

"Tell me about it," Billy said.

"But then I guess a lot of things aren't making sense, right?"

Billy thought about how he'd been spared a couple of times now.

About what that Liberator said.

It's just orders…

Why?

Why were they ordering the Liberators to spare him?

"I'd love to figure shit out," Billy said. "But we can speculate 'til we're blue in the face once we're out of here. Now come on. Enough talking. Let's…"

He saw the end of the alleyway that led onto the road up ahead, and he froze.

"Billy?" Marco said. "What's…"

And then he stopped speaking.

"Oh," he said.

He'd seen it too.

He'd seen *exactly* what Billy had seen.

Escaping this place wasn't going to be straightforward.

Of course it wasn't.

CHAPTER THIRTEEN

Billy stared at the road ahead, and his stomach sank.

The clouds were thickening above, and the hellish red of before had transformed into a familiar British grey. Everything seemed silent now. Or at least far quieter than before. There were no screams anymore. There were no gunshots anymore. And that was haunting. Because Billy knew what it meant.

Death.

There were no sounds at all, other than one sound that stood out in the silence.

Footsteps.

In the street ahead, he saw Liberators.

Lots of Liberators.

The ones from the slope, who he'd seen heading this way, down towards Eastbrook.

They were here.

He watched them march down the street, staring straight ahead, speechless. There were so many of them. Had to be hundreds.

And just seeing how many of them there were made Billy feel

totally deflated. Because sure, he knew there were a lot of these people. It wasn't like they'd appeared out of nowhere.

But at the same time... just seeing them here, seeing how many of them there were, he felt his hope slipping away.

Because he had no idea how he was going to handle these people.

Not only sneak out of Eastbrook and escape them.

But actually *handle* them, too.

Do something about them.

Protect other communities from them before they fell like this place.

Destroy them so they never made any community suffer like this ever again.

Fulfil his promise to Steve.

Fighting for Eastbrook.

He watched them march down the street, and he stood there with Marco by his side, Rex at his feet. None of them looked towards him. None of them turned their heads. It was like they all had orders to face ahead. To not turn, not even an inch.

Billy had to hope it stayed that way.

Because if they saw him, Marco, and Rex, they were in big trouble.

As for him?

Well. He had no idea what sort of fate was in store. Not anymore.

But he didn't think his luck would last forever.

"We need to... we need to hide, Billy," Marco said.

Billy heard Marco's cracking voice, and he knew he was right. They had to hide. Because escaping this place was going to be nigh-on impossible right now. Escaping was going to be unthinkable. There was only one clear route out of this place, and that was blocked by an absolute shit ton of Liberators.

If only they'd made a break from this place sooner, maybe they would've stood a chance...

But no. If he could do things differently, he wouldn't.

Because Rex was by his side.

Rex was by his side, Marco was still alive, and they still had a chance to survive.

It wasn't going to be easy. But they had to keep on taking things one step at a time.

They had to keep on hoping for the best.

Praying for the best.

Billy watched that sea of Liberators continuing to march along the street, still in disbelief about how fucking many of them there were, and he knew they couldn't take their chances by standing around here much longer.

"Come on," Billy said. "We've got to go back."

He backed up. Marco backed up. Even Rex backed up but kept his focus on the Liberators, too, like even he couldn't wrap his head around what the hell was happening and who the hell these people were.

"Any ideas *where* we're gonna hide?" Marco asked.

"I thought the whole hiding thing was your idea."

"I mean, we can find a nice cupboard under some stairs and hope for the best. But I'm not sure I fancy taking my chances with that again."

"Me neither," Billy said.

He stood at the edge of the alleyway and stared down its full length. He could hear those footsteps marching along the road, just as disturbing as the explosions and the screams they'd replaced. He gripped onto his rifle tightly. He had to be ready to use it. Couldn't dick around here. As much as he felt weak and outnumbered next to the masses of Liberators, it was something. A safety net if nothing else.

"Either way, we can't stand around here," Billy said. "Let's get going."

They ran back down the alleyway. Billy felt absolutely

exhausted at this point. Like a weight was pressing down on his shoulders, making it even more difficult to run.

And he didn't expect it would get any easier any time soon.

"We could try your place again," Marco said. "Wait in the lounge until we spot a gap, and then go for it."

Billy shook his head. "I was thinking more about taking a left."

"A left? Over the fence?"

"You see a much better route?"

"I dunno, Billy. It's risky. Hop over there and end up in the sewers. Maybe make it to the underpass if we're lucky. But even if we do... that underpass might take us right up in the middle of those creeps. I don't think that's such a good idea."

"And the houses are a much better idea? All it takes is for one of 'em to step inside, and it's over."

"I dunno. It seems like the lesser of two evils. Like..."

He stopped.

Or maybe he didn't. Billy couldn't really tell.

But everything seemed to stand still.

Time itself seemed to stand still.

Because up ahead, Billy saw something that filled his body with fear.

A familiar sight.

A sight that he should've expected.

But a sight that was terrifying all the same.

"Whatever we decide," Marco said. "We'd better decide really fucking fast."

Marco was right.

Because Liberators were in the alleyway ahead.

And they were in the alleyway behind.

They were surrounded.

CHAPTER FOURTEEN

"Okay," Marco said. "We'd better make our minds up here. Fast."

Billy saw the Liberators approaching, and he knew Marco was right. They were flooding down the end of the alleyway ahead of them. And they were flooding into the alleyway behind, too. If they stood here and twiddled their thumbs, they'd be dead in no time.

Well. Marco and Rex almost certainly would.

Him?

He didn't know. Maybe they'd spare him, just like they'd been sparing him already.

But he didn't want to know what they were sparing him for.

What they were keeping him alive for.

Or how much longer he'd get lucky.

He looked over at the houses to his right. The yards alongside him. There was no point going in there. Because they were rumbled. The Liberators were onto them. They had to get out onto the street somehow, and they had to get out of here, and going into those yards and into the houses was like climbing into their own coffins and waiting to be buried alive.

"Billy!" Marco shouted.

Billy looked at the tall metal fence right beside him. He knew it wasn't going to be an easy option. He knew they could end up going into the sewers and then into the underpass and end up trapped down there, too.

But right now, it felt like the best of two options.

Two terrible options.

Only issue?

Getting the hell over that fence before the Liberators got to them.

"We've got to go over," Billy said.

"Seriously?" Marco said. "That's seriously your plan right now—"

"Come with me or don't come with me. I'd rather you do, but if you don't, that's on you. Just… just at least give me a hand lifting my fat lump of a dog over the fence."

Marco shook his head and sighed. "Suppose you've not left me with much choice. Piling the animal guilt on my shoulders."

"Good lad," Billy said.

He put the rifle to one side, reached down, and grabbed Rex's front end. Marco crouched and lifted his back end. Rex just hovered there, wagging his docked tail, drooling all over, and licking Billy's face like this was all just some kind of big game. All the while, the Liberators surged closer.

"You hang in there, boy. You've got a little bit of a drop to come. Don't you worry. You'll be fine."

He stretched up, lifting Rex with all his strength, Marco stretching alongside him, too.

Pushing him higher, and higher, and higher.

Pushing him until they were so close to the top of the fence.

The Liberators still marching towards them.

Still filling the alleyway.

But not firing.

Still not firing.

For how long?

He had no clue. And he really didn't want to stick around to find out.

He pushed Rex higher and got himself ready to lift him over that fence when suddenly he heard something that filled him with fear.

Gunshots.

Gunshots whooshing right past him.

They were firing.

Firing at Marco.

"Shit!" Marco gasped.

He dropped Rex, who tumbled down and slammed Billy in the chest.

Billy lay on the alleyway, on his back. More gunshots cracked through the alleyway. Rex's immense weight pressed down on top of him, squeezing the air from his lungs.

"Shit," Billy said. "Shitting hell. Marco?"

He looked up, and he saw something that filled him with fear.

Or rather, what he *didn't* see filled him with fear.

Marco was gone.

There was no sign of him in the alleyway anymore.

There was no sign of him *anywhere*.

Billy and Rex were alone together.

And those Liberators were storming towards him.

He dragged himself to his feet. Stood there with Rex by his side. He looked up at the fence, and he knew he needed to get over there. The houses were a no go at this point. Over the fence was the only option.

But it wasn't exactly an appealing option; that was for goddamned sure.

He looked up at that fence, and he knew he had no time to waste.

He had to get Rex over there.

And he had to climb over after him.

"Right," he said. "Let's see how well I can lift you, you fat lump."

He grabbed Rex and lifted him. Dragged him up towards the top of that fence.

But shit, he was heavy.

Far heavier than he imagined.

Far heavier than he ever remembered him.

Starting to regret those extra scraps he gave him at dinner, that was for sure.

He kept on straining to lift Rex up and over the fence. His knees buckling. The weight getting heavier.

"Damn it, Marco," he said. "Really picked your moment to bolt."

He pushed Rex higher and higher up the side of the fence.

The Liberators getting closer.

Still holding their fire.

"Come on," he gasped. Arms shaking. Knees buckling. "Just a little higher. Just..."

And then he felt it.

Felt Rex's weight shift over the top of the fence.

He felt him tumbling out of his hands and towards the ground on the other side of the fence.

"Yes," he said. "That's it. Good lad. Good..."

He looked down for his rifle, and he realised something.

"Shit. You crafty bastard, Marco."

The rifle was gone.

It was *frigging* gone.

Billy shook his head. Glanced up at those oncoming Liberators.

He didn't have any time to think about it or get pissed off by it.

Any time to speculate.

Any time to feel annoyed at all.

The Liberators were getting closer.

Time was running out, right before his eyes.

He stretched up.

Grabbed the top of the fence.

Dragged himself up there with all his strength.

"Come on," he muttered. "Come on…"

He felt something then. A sharp pain right across his right hand.

The old stab wound in his palm.

Opening.

Bleeding out over the metal.

"Shit," Billy said. "You've got this. Come on. You've got this. Just a little further."

He stretched himself further up to the top of the fence and saw the first of the Liberators just metres away.

He dragged himself up and over the top.

Felt the fence's sharp edges digging into his body, splitting through his clothes, piercing his skin.

He didn't have time to steady himself.

He just rolled over the top.

Tumbled down to the ground below.

Hit it with a thud.

He lay there a few seconds, his head spinning.

Mouth full of the taste of blood.

And then he felt Rex's tongue against his face.

"Rex," Billy said. "You're okay. You're…"

Only there was a problem.

Rex was sitting.

He wasn't budging.

He must've hurt his paws or his legs in the fall.

Shit.

Shit, shit, shit.

He crouched down, lifted Rex's weight again, and stood.

Heart racing.

Body shaking.

Feeling weak, battered, bruised, and almost completely out of strength.

And through the fence, he saw something that filled him with fear.

The Liberators were standing there.

They didn't have their rifles raised.

They were just staring at him.

Watching him.

He had so many questions. So many things he wanted to ask them. So many things he wanted to scream at them for the pain they'd caused. For the horrors, they'd committed. For the devastation they'd brought to his community.

"What do you want?" he gasped. "What... what do you want?"

The Liberators just stared at him.

Wordless.

And as much as Billy wanted an answer, he couldn't stick around for this.

"Come on, Rex. Let's... let's get out of here."

He took a deep breath, lifted Rex up, and he ran into the woods, away from the fence, and into the unknown.

CHAPTER FIFTEEN

Billy carried Rex through the woods, but he wasn't sure how much longer he was going to be able to hold his weight.

It felt dark in the wooded area behind the houses. A little bit of a wasteland area, basically. Every now and then, Billy saw deflated footballs lying on their side from years ago. Old beer cans, rusting away, chewed up by the elements. It wasn't a large area. But it was the safest area he could be right now.

Especially when the Liberators were close.

Very, very close.

He stared at the ground as he waded through the tall grass. There was a manhole cover somewhere around here, which would lead him right down into the sewers. And sure, sewers weren't exactly top of his list of places to go right now. The last time he'd been fleeing enemies via the sewers, he'd discovered Steve was his father, that he'd been having a years-long affair with his mother, and that the man he called Dad wasn't his dad at all.

So yeah. A little understandable reluctance when it came to sewers, that was for sure. Couldn't exactly hold it against him.

He traipsed further through the grass. Still no sign of that manhole cover. Fuck, it was around here somewhere; he was sure of it.

His arms ached with Rex's weight. Poor dog, panting away. He'd really hurt his paws or his legs after the fall over the fence. It was a long way for a dog to fall. Especially an old dog like him.

He gritted his teeth, and he tasted blood.

His back ached. His legs ached. *Everywhere* ached.

But he didn't have time to mope.

He could only keep powering on.

He kept on searching the tall grass for a sign of that manhole cover. But he couldn't stop thinking about Marco. One moment he was there, holding Rex's rear end as they lifted him over the fence. The next, he was being fired at, and he was dropping Rex.

And then he was gone.

With the rifle.

He looked over his shoulder. Over towards that metal fence. Wherever Marco had got to, he hoped he was okay.

But if he hadn't climbed over the fence—which didn't seem likely—he didn't hold much hope.

He walked further through the tall grass when suddenly he felt something hollow echo beneath his feet.

He looked down.

Tapped his foot again.

And again, it echoed.

Something hollow.

Something metal.

Something that could only be one thing.

He crouched down, lowering Rex to his side, and dragged some of the tall grass away. God, he'd never been so excited about finding the entrance to a sewer before, that was for sure.

He yanked the grass away and saw the brown, rusting metal of the manhole cover staring up at him.

He stroked the cover. Smiled. "Hello, gorgeous."

He went to lift the cover when he heard something.

Rustling.

Rustling in the trees beside him.

He looked around. Didn't see any movement. Didn't hear anything else.

"Just in your head," Billy said. "All in your head."

He went to lift that manhole cover again when he saw something move in the corner of his eye.

He looked up again.

And again, he didn't see a thing.

Again, no movement whatsoever.

Only this time...

Rex was growling.

He looked around at Rex. Saw him staring in the direction of the movement. Ears raised.

Deep, nasty growl.

He took a deep breath, and he stroked Rex's fur. "Come on. The sooner we get down here, the better. And besides. I need to figure out how the hell I'm gonna get you down there with me without breaking you completely."

He pulled the manhole cover aside. A delicious smell of ancient sewage filled his nostrils, knocking him dizzy.

"Ideal," he said. "Just what we need right now."

He grabbed Rex. Lifted him. And then, somehow, he managed to clamber down the slippery old metal ladders with him—being sure to close the manhole cover over him. Surrounding them both in darkness.

The further he got down into the sewer, the worse the stench got. It wasn't going to be a fun trip, that was for sure. He just had to keep telling himself he wouldn't be in here for long. That he just had to get through to the next ladder, then climb up and out near the underpass.

And once he was in the underpass... he could try to make his way out of Eastbrook.

The whole finding other survivors thing?

It wasn't something he wanted to give up on. The thought of giving up on it felt like a total failure.

But what the hell else was he supposed to do?

He climbed further down the ladder and then felt the slippery floor beneath his feet.

"That's it," he said. "Another hurdle down. If only you could bloody walk, hmm? Absolutely knackering my back here."

Rex let out a little whimper that made Billy feel guilty right away.

Billy looked around. Which was a bit of a pointless exercise, really, because it was absolutely pitch black. So dark he couldn't see his hand in front of his face.

But he figured just as long as he stuck as close to the wall as possible, he'd find his way to the next step of ladders.

Getting Rex up there?

That was going to be a whole different matter entirely.

But again. One step at a time, right?

He started to walk along the pathway, into the pitch black and into the darkness, when suddenly he heard something behind him.

Something that sounded like footsteps.

Something that sounded like... crying?

He spun around. Squinted into the pitch black.

But he couldn't see anything.

Couldn't see a fucking thing.

"Come on, Rex," he said. "Let's get the hell out of this shithole."

He walked off, into the darkness, following the wall as closely as he could.

And then he heard it.

Right behind him.

Making the hair on the back of his neck stand right on end.

Footsteps.

CHAPTER SIXTEEN

Billy heard the footsteps, and he froze.

He stood there in the pitch-black darkness of the sewers. He couldn't see a thing, which made everything a whole lot scarier. The darkness was scary enough as it was at the best of times. When your home was amid an invasion by a ruthless band of enemies? Yeah. Yeah, it was even more fucking scary.

He looked back into the darkness towards those footsteps. Didn't seem to be many of them, whoever they were. Come to think of it... it sounded like there was just one person.

And in a way, Billy found that even scarier.

It felt like someone was stalking him in the shadows.

A monster.

Ready to rise up from the stench and swallow him whole.

The sewers smelled absolutely revolting. A rotting stench filled the stuffy air. He could taste a whole host of awful things. Blood on his lips. Sergeant Kirk's blood.

He thought of those innards spilling out of his belly, lying there like dead eels, and a shudder crept down his spine.

He tightened his grip on Rex, whose heavy weight flopped

down in his arms. He looked into the darkness, and he waited. He couldn't hear footsteps anymore. Couldn't hear *anything* anymore.

Maybe it was all in his head.

Maybe it was all completely in his imagination.

"Come on, lad," he said. "No point… no point sticking around. Better get going."

He turned around and walked away with Rex in his arms. Tried not to slip on the sewer floor. Last place he wanted to end up was that pit of shit beside him. He'd spent enough time swimming in sewer water for a lifetime, that was for sure.

Reminded him of his reunion with Steve. Or rather, the big moments he discovered Steve was his dad, all those years ago.

And then it dawned on him again.

Shit.

Steve.

Dad.

He was gone.

He was gone, and he wasn't coming back.

Billy walked further into the darkness. His arms were aching so much from hauling Rex's weight and everything else that'd gone down that he didn't think he would be able to carry him much further.

And getting him up the ladder?

Into the underpass?

Fuck. That didn't sound appealing right now.

He thought about the route this sewer ran. There was no way he could keep on going because eventually he'd hit a dead end, and he'd be forced to get in the water and swim.

And getting in the water and swimming really was the last thing he fancied doing right now.

Especially with a lame dog in his arms.

He walked further into the darkness, feeling completely and utterly blind, when suddenly he heard it again.

The footsteps.

The footsteps right behind him.

Right behind him.

He looked around into the dark. He didn't see anything. His heart pounded. Anxiety crept up inside him again.

There was somebody here in the darkness with him.

Following him.

Stalking him.

He stood there with Rex in his arms, and he wanted to say something. Because what difference would it make? Whoever was following him knew he was here, and he knew *they* were here.

But still... saying anything still felt like a risk right now.

He stood completely still and stared into the darkness, and he knew he couldn't just stand here and say nothing.

"Who... who's there?"

No response.

Just his voice echoing in the tunnel.

Billy swallowed a lump in his dry throat. Heart beating a little faster now.

"Who... who is it? What do you want?"

"Billy?" a voice said.

The hairs on the back of his neck stood right on end.

A voice. A child's voice.

He hesitated. Waited a few seconds. His heart racing even faster, somehow. His stomach turning.

"What... Who is it?"

He heard the footsteps walking right up to him.

So close to him, he could feel the heat from their body now.

A kid?

"Who is it?" Billy repeated. Thoroughly fucking creeped out, that was for sure.

"Sophie," the voice said. "I'm... I'm scared."

Sophie? Who the hell was...

But then suddenly, it clicked into place.

Sophie. Little blonde kid. Daughter of Gary, one of the engineers. Nice kid. Quiet. Smart for her age.

It was her. No doubt about it.

"Sophie," Billy said. Feeling pretty fucking relieved to find someone else alive, he had to admit. "Are you... Are you okay?"

"I'm... I saw them shooting people. Mum. And—and Dad. I ran away. I'm scared, Billy. I don't want to die like the others."

Billy crouched down, and he lay Rex down right beside him. He reached out his hands, and then out of nowhere, he felt Sophie's cold little hands in his.

"You aren't going to die," Billy said. "You don't... you don't have to worry about a thing. We're going to get out of here, okay? We're going to get out of here, and everything's going to be okay."

"You promise?" Sophie asked.

And Billy didn't want to. He didn't want to make a false promise to this girl. He didn't want to promise her something he wasn't sure he could deliver.

But then he remembered the promise he'd made to Steve as he lay dying.

The promise he'd made to fight for this community.

To fight for *everyone*.

"I promise," Billy said, his voice cracking as he spoke.

And then this kid he barely knew did something he wasn't expecting.

She leaned in.

Hugged him.

Pressed her warm, damp face against his.

"Thank you," she said. Holding him tight. "Thank you, Billy."

He wrapped his arms around her, and he held her, too. And he found his eyes welling up. The devastation above ground. The number of people who'd been slaughtered completely indiscriminately.

People like Sophie.

Like Sophie's parents.

So many people.

He held on to Sophie. And as much as he wanted to stay here in this awful shithole, hugging her forever, he knew they were going to have to get moving.

He backed away. Squeezed her shoulder. "Come on," he said. "We've... we've got to get out of here. And somehow, we've got to figure out how to carry this fat lump of a dog out of here, too. You up to the task?"

She let out a little laugh, which was so fucking nice to hear in this literal hellish moment.

And that was something he had to fight for.

If it was one person he saved or if it was fifty, this was what he had to fight for.

"Well then," he said. "Let's get to it..."

He started to lift Rex when suddenly, he saw something that filled him with terror.

A beam of light, out of nowhere, right at the end of the sewers he'd come from.

And then, the sound of footsteps echoing down the ladders.

His stomach sank.

His body tensed up.

And that sense of urgency inside him awoke again.

The Liberators were here.

CHAPTER SEVENTEEN

Billy heard the Liberators' footsteps climbing down the ladder, and he knew he needed to get the fuck out of here—fast.

He stared at the beam of light that shone down through the manhole cover the Liberators were climbing from. It still wasn't enough to lighten up the sewers, to help him see anyone or anything.

All he could focus on were the footsteps echoing down the ladders.

The sound of his own heartbeat racing in his chest.

The smell of sewage water and blood on his dry, chapped lips.

And the anxiety.

The crippling anxiety and the devastating exhaustion of being pushed back, again and again.

He had a feeling he was going to be okay. That for whatever reason, the Liberators weren't opening fire at him.

But that still didn't mean he was safe.

It didn't mean he was off the hook completely.

And besides.

Sophie.

Rex.

The Liberators weren't showing as much mercy where they were concerned, that was for sure.

"Come on," he said, grabbing Sophie's hand and dragging her down the tunnel into the darkness, trying to carry Rex's immense weight in his other hand. He knew he wouldn't be able to carry him for long. And he *certainly* wouldn't be able to haul him up a ladder and out of here.

But what the fuck else was he supposed to do?

He couldn't go back. The Liberators were already in the sewers.

And he couldn't go into the water, either. He didn't know his way out of this place. Not in the way Steve knew his sewers all those years ago.

He knew there was only one way he could go right now.

Only one thing he could do right now.

He had to run.

And he had to hope for the best.

For a miracle.

He ran further through the sewers, Rex's weight dragging down his left arm and Sophie's hand in his right, gripping it tightly. He could hear her crying. Hear her breathing rapidly. Hear her sobbing.

And he wanted to tell her it would be okay. That everything would be okay.

That he was going to keep his promise.

But he couldn't.

He couldn't pretend everything was going to be okay right now.

Because he really didn't know if it was.

Especially not with those Liberators closing in.

"We're okay," he said. "Almost there. We'll be okay. Almost there."

He ran and ran further down the slippery pathway. He had to

be careful. Rex's weight might just drag him into the water, and if he fell in there, he didn't feel like he had the strength to get himself out.

"Almost there, Sophie," he said, keeping on going, praying he felt the bottom of the ladder soon. "Almost there."

He heard the footsteps behind him, getting closer.

He heard those Liberators closing in.

"I'll get you out of here," he gasped. "I'll get you out of here, and everything'll be okay. I promise everything'll be okay..."

And then he felt it.

The ladder.

The ladder right by his side.

"Here," he said. "We're here."

He looked back. Saw the Liberators' silhouettes running towards them.

And then he looked up at that ladder in the darkness before him, and he knew what he needed to do.

He knew he only had one choice.

"Sophie. Listen to me. And listen very closely. You're... you're going to have to climb the ladder. You're going to have to get up there, and you're going to have to push that hatch aside. And you're... you're going to have to run. Okay? You're going to have to run. Don't stop for anyone. Or for anything. Just... just get yourself out of here and run. And believe in yourself, okay? Believe... believe that you're strong. Because you *are* strong. Okay? You are strong. And don't ever believe anything else."

Sophie was quiet for a few seconds. "But what—what about you and Rex?"

"We'll be right behind you," he lied. A lump swelling in his throat. "Okay? We'll be right behind you. And... and we'll be with you. Always."

He put a hand on Sophie's shoulder as those footsteps got closer and closer, so close now.

"Go, Sophie," he said. "Go. Now."

And then he felt her hug him.

Felt her wrap her arms around him again and tighten them.

"Thank you," she said.

And then she turned, and Billy heard her feet echoing against the ladder.

He heard her gasping.

Heard her struggling.

Heard her climbing away.

And as he listened to that sound getting quieter and quieter, more and more distant, he felt happiness.

A deep, bittersweet sense of happiness.

She was going to be okay.

He knew deep down in his bones that she was going to be okay.

He closed his burning eyes.

Turned around, Rex still in his arms, panting away.

Looked at the darkness ahead.

At those approaching footsteps.

"Well, boy," he said. "It looks like it's just you and me again now, hmm?"

Rex licked his face with his slobbery tongue.

And Billy didn't push him away like he usually did.

He let him.

Savoured every fucking second.

He stood there and stared at the darkness as the Liberators got closer.

As their echoing footsteps stopped, right before him.

And he held his breath and waited for whatever was about to unfold.

It was time.

CHAPTER EIGHTEEN

Billy stood in the darkness of the sewers with Rex in his arms and waited for the Liberators to make their next move.

It was pitch black, other than that beam of light in the distance, where the Liberators had pulled the manhole cover aside and climbed down. He could see their dark silhouettes, too. Their dark silhouettes standing right opposite him, right in front of him. He could hear water dripping into the river of shit, echoing all around this place. It reeked so frigging bad that he thought he might just pass out at any moment.

But even though he knew he was trapped, he felt happy.

Because he knew Sophie was okay.

She was climbing the ladder.

She was going to get out of here, and she was going to be okay.

He stood there, Rex in his arms, and took deep breaths of this awful, stuffy air, and he waited for the Liberators to do whatever they wanted to do.

But they didn't do anything.

They didn't say a word.

They didn't move another muscle.

They just stood there, right before him, in the darkness.

He looked at their silhouettes.

Looked from one of them to the next.

He waited for them to say something. To do something. Anything.

But the longer he waited, the more he realised they weren't going to do anything at all.

They were waiting for him to make his move.

"What... what are you... what do you want?"

His voice echoed through the sewers.

The Liberators were silent.

"You come into my home," Billy said. "You slaughter my people. And now you don't even have the decency to tell me why the fuck you're doing what you're doing. So go on. Tell me. Fucking tell me. What do you want? And why are you..."

He heard a scream.

Above him.

Looked up.

And instinctively, he knew what was happening.

Sophie.

She was falling.

He staggered back, stood at the bottom of the ladder, and then he felt her slam into his face, trainer first, knocking him off balance.

But he cushioned her fall.

Stopped her tumbling down to the solid floor below—and to certain death.

He held her as well as he could. And then he eased her down. Pushed her behind him, standing in front of her. Blocking her from the Liberators' view. Fuck. She was supposed to be out of here by now. She wasn't supposed to be here.

She was supposed to be long gone.

He looked at the dark silhouettes of the Liberators standing right in front of him. Standing there, totally speechless, not saying a word.

"You leave her alone, okay? Whatever weird, fucked up rules you have for me, and for whatever reason... you leave her alone."

More silence.

Billy's heart beating faster and faster.

"What do you want?" he shouted. "What do you—"

"We wanted to spare you because they were our orders," someone said. A voice. Gruff. Deep. Out of nowhere. "And we honour our agreements."

Silence.

Silence followed the man's words.

Words Billy was surprised to even *hear*, in all truth.

"But you have proven... difficult. And for that reason, you've left us with no choice."

He saw the silhouettes of the rifles lifting.

Saw them pointing at him.

At Rex.

And at Sophie.

"Please," Billy said. "Whatever fucked up reasons you have for doing this... we're people. We're people, just like you—"

"On your knees. Make it easier for yourself."

"I..."

And then Billy felt something.

Sophie.

Squeezing his leg.

Holding on for dear life.

He looked down at the darkness where he would be, and then he crouched down beside her.

He crouched beside her, and he stroked her tear-soaked face.

"I'm scared, Billy. I'm scared."

"You don't have to be scared," Billy said. "I promised—I promised everything was going to be okay. Didn't I?"

"But these people—"

"Don't worry about these people. I've got you. Okay? I've got you. As long as you—as long as you hold on tight, everything's going to be okay. As long as you—you stroke Rex, everything's going to be alright. Okay?"

He looked up at the dark silhouettes where the Liberators stood.

He looked up at them, and he felt hatred.

Total hatred.

Because they had destroyed his community.

They had destroyed his home.

And they had destroyed all the amazing people in this place.

"You'll remember this," Billy said. "You might not feel it now. But one night, you'll wake up, and you'll remember the things you've done. You'll see the people you've killed. And if you have any fucking conscience about you, you'll suffer for what you've done."

Silence.

Total silence.

And then, "Any last words?" The gruff voice again.

Billy looked up as he held on to Sophie.

As he stroked Rex.

He looked up at the firing squad before him, and then he closed his eyes.

"I'm sorry I couldn't do more, Steve," he said. "I'm sorry I couldn't do more, Dad. But I... I hope you know I did everything I could."

He kept his eyes closed.

Felt the warmth of Sophie's body against his.

Felt Rex's soft fur under his hand.

"I'm sorry," he said. "I..."

And then he heard the gunshots.

CHAPTER NINETEEN

Billy heard the gunshots.

Not for the first time, he waited for the splitting pain to spread across his body.

For the thump of the bullets into his chest, into his stomach, into his head.

He waited for all these things, but it wasn't *him* he thought of.

It was Sophie.

Sophie hiding right behind him.

And Rex.

Rex lying right beside him.

He thought of Sophie, and he thought of Rex, and he waited for the pain to spread through his body.

But also not for the first time... he didn't feel any pain.

He didn't feel *anything*.

Even though he could hear the bullets firing, echoing through the sewers, he didn't feel a thing.

He opened his eyes.

Light.

Flashes of light filling the darkness.

Bullets smacking into the brick walls and thumping into the stagnant water.

He watched the darkness illuminating before him.

Knelt right there, holding on to Sophie, holding on to Rex.

He knelt there, and he watched as the darkness flashed, again, and again, and again.

The gunshots so loud, so deafening.

He watched, and he waited, and then the darkness deepened again.

The gunshots stopped.

The flashes stopped.

Silence.

Billy knelt there. Heart thumping. Rex resting his head on his lap. Sophie squeezing hold of him tight.

His ears rang. He couldn't hear anything other than that loud ringing. If someone were speaking or even screaming right now, he wouldn't be able to hear them.

He stared into the darkness, and he tried to understand what'd just happened. Tried to wrap his head around whatever the fuck had just gone down.

And then he saw movement.

Movement, right ahead.

Movement, walking towards him.

A silhouette.

Just one silhouette.

Heading right his way.

He held on to Sophie, held on to Rex. He had no idea what'd just gone down. No idea what that cacophony of gunfire was all about.

Only that he wasn't sure he'd ever hear a damned thing again after that.

He stared up at that dark silhouette, when out of nowhere, light blinded him.

A bright light from the torch of whoever was before him.

The Liberator before him.

He covered his face with his hand. Squinted. Still absolutely frigging terrified.

But also... wondering.

Why was there only one silhouette now?

What were all the gunshots about?

He moved his hand away from his face and squinted into the blinding light, which wasn't much better than the suffocating darkness just moments ago.

He stood up. Slowly. Kept Sophie behind him. And held on to Rex. He didn't want to let him go. He didn't want to let either of them go.

And then he stepped towards that Liberator.

Slowly.

One step at a time.

Just one step at a time.

He walked towards the light and stopped, right opposite this silhouette. A man's silhouette, clearly.

He looked right at him. Right into the darkness.

"Who are you?" Billy asked.

The man could've been saying anything right now. Billy still couldn't hear. His hearing was totally fucked.

But he saw the man turn the torch around on the floor.

And Billy saw bodies.

Fallen bodies of Liberators.

Gunshots in their heads.

Blood spitting out of their necks.

Dead.

Billy looked up at the man, still hidden in the darkness. "Marco?" he said. "Is that you?"

The man kept the torch on the floor.

His identity still hidden.

"I can't... I can't wait around here much longer. Who the hell are..."

And then the man did something that stopped Billy in his tracks.

He turned the torch.

Shone it right up at his own face.

Billy stepped back.

Squinted at this man.

Trying to figure out who he was or what he was showing him.

One thing was for sure. It wasn't Marco.

It wasn't anyone he recog...

Wait.

No.

Wait a second.

It *was* somebody he recognised.

Somebody he recognised very well.

"You," Billy said. "It's... it's you."

CHAPTER TWENTY

Tristan Harper stood opposite the man called Billy, and he knew he'd made the biggest gamble of his entire fucking life.

He stood in the darkness of the sewers. Billy stood opposite him, illuminated by his torch. Beside him, a dog, and behind him, this little girl.

And there was something about this little girl.

She reminded him of someone.

A girl from a long time ago.

One he'd shot the parents and brother of, one after another.

One he'd let go.

The first crack in his certainty about the General's orders.

The crack that had been splitting right up to today.

He looked down into her bright blue eyes, and he knew he was weak for succumbing to mercy. For letting himself stray from his true purpose and his people's true, noble goal.

But he just couldn't do this anymore.

He just couldn't.

He thought about the General's orders, and he shivered.

He thought about what the General and the rest of his people would do to him if they found out about his betrayal.

It made him feel sick. Very sick.

But at least he could feel *something*.

At least he wasn't numb.

Not anymore.

Even if the main emotion that replaced the numbness was a crippling agony and guilt about the things he'd done.

The crimes he'd committed.

The pain he'd caused.

He stood there, the sound of his gunshots ringing in his ears, and he took a deep breath of this awful air. It smelled like the time his uncle Kenny had food poisoning on holiday in Wales, back when he was a young kid. He'd never forget being trapped inside that caravan with him, listening to his insides explode, listening to him heave, and the fear it instilled in him. The fear of hearing anyone vomit. The fear of hearing *anyone* suffer.

And the smell.

That god-awful smell...

He looked at Billy, and he swallowed a lump in his throat.

There was no time to explain to Billy what'd just happened or why he'd just done what he'd just done.

Only that deep down, he knew it was right.

Deep down, he knew there was no other choice. Not really.

Deep down, he knew it was the only thing he could've done.

Like everything had built towards this moment.

Everything.

"We need to get out of here," he said. "Right now."

Billy just stared at him. Wide-eyed. So too did the kid. Even the dog seemed bemused about all this. "I know you. But... but who the hell are you? And why are you helping?"

"I'm Tristan. The rest doesn't matter right now. We need to get out of here. Immediately."

Tristan looked over his shoulder. Back towards the manhole opening he'd climbed down.

And he remembered following his team down those ladders.

He remembered following them into the darkness.

He remembered lifting the rifles and pointing them at Billy, the girl, and the dog and thinking, "No."

Sometimes in life, you find yourself at a fork in the road.

And sometimes in life, you have to trust your instincts over your logic.

You have to trust your gut.

"I know you don't trust me," Tristan said. "And rightly so. I can't... I can't promise you anything. I can't promise you'll live. I certainly can't promise anyone else has survived. But I can promise you I'll do what I can. To—to help you get away from this place."

Billy looked back at him. Shaking his head now. Staring at him like he was an alien. A monster. A look Tristan was used to.

"Why now?" Billy asked.

"What?"

"All these people. All this death. Why... why now? What's changed?"

Tristan heard those words, and he felt a sadness weighing down deep in his body.

Why now?

Because Billy was right. He was responsible for so many horrible things. Fuck, the word "horrible" didn't do it anywhere near enough justice.

He'd murdered so many people. And it didn't matter how old they were. What gender they were. It didn't matter how much they pleaded, how much they begged.

He'd seen horrible things. Colleagues of his raping the bodies of those begging for their lives.

Or raping the bodies of the dead while their children looked on.

And all that time, he was supposed to believe he was the good person?

That this was just war, and sometimes people did awful things to further a good cause?

He was really supposed to believe that?

He looked at Billy, and he really wanted to answer him, but at the same time, he knew time was running out.

He knew they didn't have much time at all.

Soon, someone would be down here to check on him and his colleagues. Especially after the gunfire.

And Tristan really didn't want to be caught with a rifle in hand and the bodies of his colleagues around him when that happened.

"You're going to do exactly as I say," Tristan said. "You're going to dress up like one of us. You're going to grab a rifle and—and you're going to make yourself blend in. The girl... the girl goes over your shoulder. The dog goes over mine. Or vice versa—"

"You're not touching either of them."

"I'm trying to help you—"

"You're not fucking laying your hands on either of them. Understand?"

Tristan nodded, sighed. "Look. If we want to stand a chance of getting away from here, we're going to have to blend in. And then, when the right moment arrives... we make a break for it. But you need to understand what that means. It means never coming back here. It means your home is gone. And it means... it means that no matter what happens, you're going to be on the run from my people for the rest of your life. Both of us are. Because that's just how it is now. Trust me. I'm... I was one of them up until pretty recently. Up until I bailed you out in the kitchen earlier. So I would know."

Billy looked right into Tristan's eyes. Squinted. Like he was trying to figure Tristan out. A look Tristan often saw staring back at him in the mirror all the goddamned time.

"But we don't have any time to waste. You know that as well as

I do. You get changed. And we try this. It might work. It might not. But it's the best chance we've got. Believe me. Understand?"

Billy looked around at the kid.

He looked at his dog.

And then he looked up at Tristan and asked him a question Tristan really didn't want to answer.

"Why aren't they shooting me?"

Tristan lowered his head. Felt his heartbeat picking up.

He wasn't qualified to answer that question.

He didn't have time to go there.

He didn't think Billy would want to hear it. Not right now.

"Hey," Billy said. Squaring right up to him. "If I let you help us, you're going to need to answer my question. No beating around the bush. What is it they want with me?"

Tristan looked Billy in the eye, and he knew he wasn't going to give up without some kind of answer.

"Why can't you just be straight with me?" Billy asked. "Why can't you..."

And then he stopped.

And Tristan knew why right away.

The manhole cover directly above them opened, filling the sewers with light.

They weren't alone.

CHAPTER TWENTY-ONE

Billy saw the light right above them, and he knew they were completely and utterly fucked.

The Liberators were here. And they were climbing down the ladders through the manhole cover.

Their route out of the dark, filthy sewers was blocked.

Completely frigging blocked.

He looked around at Sophie, who cowered behind him. At Rex, lying on his stomach, wagging his tail, and panting with no bother in the world.

And then he looked at this man called Tristan, who stared up the open manhole cover with wide eyes.

"Well?" Billy said.

Tristan looked around at the bodies of his colleagues. The ones he'd shot down. Something Billy was still struggling to get his head around.

The way he'd just snapped.

The way Billy's ears were still ringing from the gunshots right now.

"Tristan," Billy muttered as those footsteps clattered further and further down the ladders. "We don't—we don't have any time to—"

"Get out of the way," Tristan said.

"What?"

"Trust me. Just... just get out of the way, okay?"

That was kind of the problem, though. Billy *didn't* trust this guy. And yet...

What other fucking option did he have right now?

He stepped back, gently pushing Sophie back along with him, while Rex just sat there like the big lump he was.

He saw Tristan staring up, his wide eyes wider than ever right now.

Saw him muttering something under his breath.

Shaking his head.

And then he walked over to the foot of the ladder, lifted his rifle, and he started firing.

Billy couldn't believe what he was witnessing.

Bodies of the Liberators, tumbling down those ladders.

One.

Two.

Three.

Falling into the sewers, their bones cracking on impact.

Choking on their own blood.

And Tristan—a man who *was* one of these people up until very fucking recently—responsible for their deaths.

He fired another couple of shots, which echoed around the sewers, and then he stopped.

Crept over to the opening.

Slowly.

Looked up.

And then he turned to Billy, and he nodded. "We're good. We're all—"

It all happened so fast.

Out of nowhere, one of those fallen Liberators grabbed Tristan by his ankle.

Yanked him down to the sewer floor.

Billy looked down at Tristan. Then over at the ladders. He had a chance to get away. A chance to escape with Sophie.

But Tristan...

Tristan was fighting. Fighting for his fucking life right now.

And there was an opening, right here before Billy.

A chance to get away.

To get Sophie and Rex away.

He saw that opportunity right before his eyes, and then he shook his head.

Tristan had saved his life.

He'd saved Sophie's life.

He couldn't leave him behind.

He ran over to one of the fallen Liberators.

Grabbed a rifle.

Pointed it to the back of the head of the man strangling Tristan.

"Hey," Billy said.

The Liberator swung around.

Looked right into Billy's eyes.

Billy tightened his finger on the trigger. "This is for my people."

And then he pulled the trigger.

The bullets slammed into the man's face.

Blood peppered everywhere from his exploding head.

Gunshots filled the sewers, making his ears ring.

The Liberator tumbled back, his face a bloody mess. Twitched on the floor, bleeding out.

He was dead. No coming back from what Billy just did to him.

Tristan lay there. Covered in this man's blood.

"Jesus," he said.

Billy held out a hand. "You can thank me later. Come on. It's about time we got the fuck out of here, don't you think?"

Tristan shook his head. Then he grabbed Billy's hand, got to his feet.

"Now," Billy said. "About disguising as them…"

"It's already too late for that," Tristan said. "Our only chance right now is to run. And to pray."

"I thought it might be. How am I going to get my dog up here?"

"Your dog?"

"Yeah. It is a dog. Unless you've spent so long losing your humanity that you've forgotten we used to keep these things as pets."

Tristan shook his head. "I—It's impossible."

"It's not fucking impossible. What's impossible is that I leave him behind. Understand?"

Tristan opened his mouth like he was going to argue, and then he sighed. "Look. We can… we can use some rope to tie him to you. But really. We don't have the time for any of this nonsense right now."

"Then you'd better get a fucking move on, hadn't you?"

Billy waited while Tristan tied the rope to him. While he tied Rex to his shoulders. Jesus Christ. He seemed even heavier on his back than he did in his arms—and he wasn't light in his arms by any fucking stretch of the imagination.

But hell, he meant it when he said what he said to Tristan. He wasn't leaving Rex behind. Because what even was the point getting out of this place if he didn't manage to save his best mate?

And there was Sophie.

He looked at Sophie, standing there in the darkness before him. Shivering. So brave.

And he forced a smile at her.

"It'll be okay," he said. "Just like I promised."

He felt Tristan tighten Rex around his body, and then he

patted his shoulder. "There. I can't guarantee it'll hold. He's a rather... weighty dog. But... but it should do. For now."

Billy nodded. He didn't want to thank Tristan. And a part of him didn't even want Tristan to come with them. He was one of the Liberators, after all. He was involved in Steve's death, and he was responsible for the deaths of so many others, too. And it didn't fucking matter that he'd just had a crisis of confidence or seen the light—he was still a butcher.

And yet... Billy had saved him.

For some reason, he'd saved him.

"Right," Billy said. "After you."

"After me?" Tristan said.

"If anyone's up there, I want it to be your head popped first. Not mine. And certainly not Sophie's."

Tristan shook his head. "It's supposed to be me helping you out here. Not you holding me hostage."

Billy lifted the rifle. "We don't have to play nicely if you don't want to."

Tristan shook his head. "Okay. Okay. Just... just stay close. When we get up there. And follow my orders. Okay?"

"We'll see about that. Get a move on."

Tristan sighed, and he started climbing the ladder. As he did, Billy crouched down. He instantly regretted it because Rex's weight meant he wasn't sure he was going to stand up again.

He looked into Sophie's eyes. "We're going to get out of this. Okay? I made you a promise. I'm going to keep it."

She looked right back at him with total trust and total faith, and then she nodded.

"Good," Billy said. "Let's get out of this place."

He turned around.

Started climbing the ladder.

Saw Tristan right above him.

Saw the beautiful light right above.

Rex panted away on his shoulders, drooling down his face. He was enjoying this far too much. "Don't get any fucking ideas," Billy said.

He heaved Rex's weight up. Looked down at Sophie, right beneath him.

"We'll make this," he said as he climbed even further. "We... we'll make this."

He saw Tristan stop.

Right above him.

Saw him waiting there.

Not quite out of the manhole cover, but right at the edge of it.

"Tristan?" Billy said.

"Just... just wait a second."

"You said there's no time to—"

"I might just be on the verge of having my head shot off my shoulders," Tristan said. "Allow me a moment. Please."

Billy gritted his teeth. Clutched onto the cold metal of the ladders with his shaking hands. Gravity—and a whole lot of Rex— threatened to drag him back down into the abyss below, taking Sophie with him.

And then Tristan spoke.

"Okay," he said.

"Okay?"

"Okay."

He dragged himself out of the manhole cover.

And as he lifted himself, Billy held his breath.

Waited for that gunshot.

Gripped on for dear life just in case he came falling down.

But that didn't happen.

Tristan climbed out of the manhole cover, and he turned around, waving Billy up. "It's clear. Come on. Hurry. We don't have much time."

Billy stretched for the next rung on the ladder. The climb growing harder and harder. "You hear that, Sophie?" he said. "We're—we're getting out of this place. It's going to be okay."

He reached for another rung.

His fingers shaking so much he wasn't sure he could hold on for another second.

"Just... just one more..."

He reached for the edge of the surface.

Grabbed it.

Held on. Tight.

Relief surging through his body.

The smell of the smoke in the air and the breeze against his skin was such a luxury compared to the humid cesspit of the sewers.

"We're going to make it," he said, squinting. "We're going to make it."

He looked up at Tristan, who reached out a hand to help him.

He looked into his eyes, and as much as he wanted to hate this man... as much as he was going to get answers from him... he'd saved him.

He'd given him a chance.

He'd given Sophie a chance.

He went to drag himself out of the sewers when suddenly he heard something.

Right behind Tristan.

Footsteps.

And then the sound of a rifle clicking.

"Not another move," a voice said.

CHAPTER TWENTY-TWO

"Not another move," a voice said.

The second Billy heard that voice, his stomach sank.

Typical. Just fucking typical.

Billy lay flat on his chest on the ground. He could smell shit in the air, festering its way up from the sewers below. A cool breeze on his face. He swore he smelled smoke in there.

A smell that made his stomach churn.

The smell of death.

But as he lay there, flat on his chest, he couldn't believe just how quiet everything was. He couldn't hear gunshots anymore. He couldn't hear shouting or crying anymore. It was like the entire community had fallen to sleep. Like someone had cast a spell over it, made it fall silent.

Either that or it was dead.

Completely dead.

He saw Tristan standing over him, eyes wide. Rifle in hand.

He felt Rex's weight pressing down on his back, crushing his lungs with his immense strength.

And he knew Sophie was hanging onto those ladders behind him.

He lay flat on his stomach as Rex's slobber drooled down onto his face, and he swallowed a lump in his throat.

Of course, someone was here.

Of course, they weren't getting out of here.

He took a deep breath, and he braced himself for whatever was heading his way when suddenly he heard the voice say something he really didn't expect.

"Billy?"

Billy frowned. That voice. It sounded familiar. Unless... shit. Maybe these people knew who he was. Maybe that's why they weren't firing at him. Maybe whoever ran these people was some nutter from his past. Nothing was off the fucking table really, was it?

But then... No. This voice. It sounded familiar. Very familiar.

He tilted his head so he could see who was standing behind Tristan, and then he saw exactly who it was.

"Marco?"

Marco stood there holding the rifle he'd snatched earlier. He had it pointed at Tristan. He looked sweaty. A few splashes of blood on his face. And a little shaky, too.

But he was alive.

Marco was actually alive.

"What the... How the hell did you..."

"Yeah," Marco said. "Don't think I've ever been this pleased to see you, either."

But he stayed put.

He kept his rifle pointed at Tristan.

"Who's this fucker?" Marco asked.

"He... he helped us."

"What?"

"I know it sounds crazy. But he helped us through the sewers. Did some... did some pretty nasty things to help us."

"And I'm supposed to just trust him all of a sudden?"

"I'm not saying to trust him. I just—"

"His people slaughtered our fucking people," Marco shouted. "They slaughtered our children. And we're supposed to just take it? We're supposed to just let him live?"

Billy looked into Tristan's eyes, and he saw the defeat on his face.

Like Tristan knew already that his fate was near.

And as Billy sat there, staring into his eyes, he felt the hatred too. He felt the detestation for this man who had been a part of such savagery. Such butchery. Such slaughter.

But at the same time...

He'd helped Billy, Rex, and Sophie escape.

He'd murdered his own people to help.

So suddenly, it felt like it didn't matter what he'd done... but mattered more what he was doing right now.

"We don't have time to stand around and deliberate," Billy said. "The Liberators are still in our home. They're still in our streets. And we have a chance here. A chance to actually..."

He stopped. Because Billy realised what he was about to say.

A chance to actually get out of here.

And he wasn't sure how it made him feel. Because his original plan was to fight these Liberators. To destroy them.

For the community.

For Steve.

But right now, seeing the smoke rising in the air, tasting the death on his lips, and knowing what the silence meant... he knew the odds didn't look good.

So as much as he didn't want to run away from home right now... he knew it might just give him the best opportunity to regroup.

To start again.

"Give me one good reason not to put a bullet through this fucker's head right now," Marco said.

Billy looked around at the manhole entrance.

"You can come up now, Sophie," he said. "It's... it's okay."

Marco frowned.

Nobody appeared.

And for a horrifying moment, as Billy lay there with Rex's full weight still pressing down onto him, slobbering all over his face, he wondered if Sophie had fallen into the sewers or something.

But then she appeared.

She climbed up. Wide-eyed. Staring over at Marco with horror on her face.

Billy turned around to Marco. "You can shoot him in the head if you want. But right in front of a little girl? A little girl who might well need this man's help to get out of this place?"

Marco shook his head. More sweat trickled down his face. "Don't make me do this, Billy."

"Then don't do it," Billy said. "I'm not saying he's forgiven. He knows that. But the truth is... he's still here with us. Even though he's armed. He's still here with us, willingly. And he wants to help us get away from here. Whatever he's done wrong... and he's done plenty wrong... we can deal with that later. For now... let's get out of here. Let's get away."

Marco looked at Billy.

Then his eyes darted to Tristan.

Then Sophie.

Then back at Tristan again.

And then Billy.

"I promise I'll do what I can to help you," Tristan said. "I don't expect your trust. I don't expect your forgiveness. But I promise I'll do what I can."

He closed his eyes.

Waited for Marco to pull the trigger.

Billy saw Marco's finger around that trigger.

Tightening.

Tightening.

He waited for the blast.

He saw the confusion on Marco's face.

The sense of conflict.

And then Marco lowered the rifle.

"Fuck," he said. "You'd better get us the hell out of here in one piece. If you don't, you're dead. Understand? Dead?"

Tristan nodded, patient as ever. "I'll do my best."

"You'd better do your fucking best. Because..."

He stopped.

He stopped because he'd heard something.

Something Billy heard too.

Footsteps.

Banging.

Getting closer.

And closer.

He looked over his shoulder.

Looked over towards the end of the street.

Saw those shadows approaching.

And then he heard Tristan say two words that sent a shiver up his spine.

"They're here."

CHAPTER TWENTY-THREE

Billy saw the shadows approaching and heard those marching footsteps, and he knew they were in the shit again.

He forced himself to his feet, Rex still weighing down heavily on his spine. Clouds thickened overhead, turning the red glow to a steely grey. Warm specks of rain trickled down from above.

He looked down the street. The empty, dead street.

Looked right to the bottom.

Heard those marching footsteps approaching.

So, so close to turning the corner and stepping around here.

And then?

They'd be fucked.

Completely and utterly fucked.

"We've got to get out of here," Billy said.

He grabbed Sophie's hand, turned, and ran as fast as he could down the street, which wasn't as fast as it would be if Rex weren't on his back. Tristan and Marco followed closely, both looking over their shoulders, both trying to see what was coming.

"We're running out of time," Tristan said.

"Yeah," Billy said. "I can see that much."

"We need... we need to get to the main gates, and we need to get out of here."

"That's your plan?" Billy said. "We keep you alive so you can help us, and that's what you've got?"

"My plan was for you to dress like one of them and blend in. But that didn't exactly go quite how we wanted it to, did it?"

"Fuck," Billy muttered. He clutched onto Rex. Tried to run, even though the load on his shoulders made it feel like he was going to fall over at any second.

He could see the turn in the road, which would soon lead out towards the main gate.

They had to go through there.

And then they had to get away.

And then?

Then could wait.

Figuring out what they had to do next could wait.

Only now mattered.

"Come on," he said, squeezing Sophie's hand. "Almost there."

He could feel her cold hand tightening around his, and it made him feel so fucking sad. Because there were so many kids like her here in Eastbrook. Innocent kids who just wanted to *be* kids.

And now, here they were. Thrown into an absolute hellscape. A group ruthlessly hunting them down for no reason at all.

So much horror.

So much death.

And still, they were having to run away.

He looked over his shoulder. He didn't want to. Really didn't want to see what the hell or who the hell was coming but figured he didn't really have a choice.

When he looked back, he saw the first of the Liberators appear.

That big block of them he'd seen walking down the road earlier.

It was them.

Tristan was right. They really *were* fucking here.

He turned back around and ran down the alleyway on the right. Raced to the bottom. *Come on. You can do this. You can make it. Almost there. Almost...*

When he reached the end of the alleyway, he stopped in his tracks.

The road ahead was crawling with Liberators.

They were blocking the main gate.

A man crouched on his knees before them. Bloodied and bruised. Palms clasped together.

"Please," he begged. "I just—I just want to get out. I don't want no trouble. I just want to—"

The blast of a rifle.

The man's head burst onto the road.

His body flopped onto the street, twitching.

The Liberator standing over him, rifle in hand.

"Fuck," Marco said. "What now?"

Billy stood there, heart racing, and he didn't know what to suggest.

They were coming from behind them.

And they were blocking the main gate.

They were trapped.

Completely trapped.

Unless...

He turned around, back to where they'd come from.

Crept to the edge of the alleyway.

"Billy?"

"The underpass," Billy said. Pointing into the distance.

"We've fucking talked about this. Have you lost your mind?" Marco asked.

"I don't see there's any other way. We go through the underpass. We get out of this place. It's the only way."

Marco's mouth widened, but no words came out.

And then he just nodded.

Shook his head and nodded.

"I don't like it. But I don't see what other choice we've got."

"Exactly," Billy said.

He stood there, holding Sophie's hand tight.

Rex panting and drooling onto his face, which reeked.

He looked down at Sophie, and he smiled at her.

"We're going to do this," he said. "We're going to be okay."

She looked into his eyes and opened her mouth.

And then she closed it.

Nodded.

"I know we will," she said.

He squeezed her hand. "Good kid. Then let's go."

They ran out onto the street, into the open. Billy didn't look back. He couldn't. He didn't want to see how close to death he was.

He saw the underpass up ahead. The place where they were to hide the vulnerable in case of emergency.

And his stomach sank when he saw the doors had already been ripped open.

When he saw the blood on the road at the side of the entrance.

The fragments of bone and the chunks of flesh.

He squeezed Sophie's hand. Limped along as quickly as he could. "Just a few more steps. Just a few more..."

Bullets.

Gunfire.

They were being shot at.

The Liberators had seen them.

"Shit."

They ran faster towards that door.

Towards that darkness.

As the bullets kept on peppering towards them.

But they were almost there.

They were almost there, and they'd get a breather.

For a moment, they'd get a breather.

And then they'd have to get through the underpass before…

No.

One step at a time.

One damned step at a time.

He reached the dark entrance to the underpass. Smelled blood in the air. Saw bodies lying all around the entrance.

Children's bodies.

He stood there, and he froze.

Sophie cried beside him.

"Close your eyes," he said. "Close your eyes, and it'll be okay. I'll lead the way."

He went to step through the underpass doors.

Marco followed closely.

He looked back, and he saw Tristan standing there, rifle in hand, staring right at Billy.

"Tristan?"

Tristan's eyes were wide. He didn't have that dead expression. Not anymore.

"Tristan? We need to go."

And then he took a deep breath, and he smiled.

"I'm no use to you. I wanted to pretend I was… but I'm not. I'm really not."

Billy frowned. The Liberators kept on coming, kept on firing. "What the hell are you…"

"Their base is in Ulston. Thirty miles from here. You can hit them where it hurts. It won't destroy them, but it will cripple them. And that's the best you can hope for. That's the best way you can hit them."

"What about you?" Billy asked.

Tristan's smile widened. A tear crawled down his cheek.

"Tristan?"

"I'll never expect forgiveness for what I've done. But if I can help you get away from this place even just a little bit... I can die knowing I did the right thing."

"What—"

"Go," Tristan shouted. "And don't you dare turn back."

He grabbed the underpass doors.

And then he pushed them.

Pushed them hard as the Liberators kept coming.

"Tristan?" Billy said.

"Go," Tristan said. "Go."

And then, with all his strength, he slammed the doors shut.

Darkness filled the underpass.

Tristan was gone.

CHAPTER TWENTY-FOUR

Billy held on to Sophie's hand as they ran through the darkness of the underpass, and he really, really didn't want to look at what was either side of him.

It was pitch black down here. And it was suffocating and claustrophobic in a different way to how the sewers were. Mostly because he knew what was either side of him.

Eyes staring up at him.

The eyes of the dead.

The eyes of those who had been slaughtered.

Shot and executed by the Liberators.

The very same Liberators who Tristan had just saved them from—again.

Or rather... bought them a little extra time from.

He ran down through the darkness. Marco wasn't far behind. He kept on hearing Marco swearing under his breath, cursing to himself. And Billy couldn't blame him. That's why he wasn't looking either side.

He didn't want to look.

He didn't want to see those eyes peering right back up at him.

He was traumatised enough by everything that had happened. And he *knew* without seeing what kind of a state things were in.

He swallowed a lump in his throat. A knot tightened in his chest.

Just keep going, Billy. Just keep your head down and keep going. It's all you can do.

He ran further down the underpass, and he knew where they had to go. They just had to follow this route.

Follow this route, then climb out the other side.

And then make a dash for it.

But judging by the signs he'd seen at the doorway—at the bodies he knew were lying beside him—the Liberators had already broken in that way. Or they'd got in somehow. Maybe that was how they'd managed to cause so much havoc and attacked with such an element of surprise.

Fuck. He hated that he was running away. Felt like a coward. A total coward.

But at the same time... he knew this was the best shot at surviving.

And the best shot at defeating the Liberators was by surviving.

He thought about what Tristan told him. That place. Ulston.

How they could go there, thirty miles away, and cripple the Liberators.

Cripple them how? He wasn't sure.

But he couldn't think too far ahead about that just yet.

His priority was still getting out of this place.

Getting away from here, and...

He felt something against his foot.

Tripped up and went flying face flat to the ground.

Landed on something... well. Not *soft* exactly. But softer than the ground.

When Billy felt the blood, he knew exactly what it was.

A body.

A small body too.

Small hands. Hands just like Sophie's.

The body of a child.

He rushed back to his feet, which wasn't as quick as he'd like it with Rex weighing down on his shoulders. It was discoveries like this that made him despise Tristan, despite everything he'd done for him in his final hours.

He was part of a machine that destroyed his community. Destroyed his home. Murdered his children.

Marco was right. He didn't sympathise with Tristan. He couldn't.

And he certainly didn't forgive him.

But at least he'd done the right thing... even if it was too little too late.

Billy looked back into the darkness. He knew that door wasn't going to be closed forever. The Liberators would find their way in here, and they'd be hunting them down again in no time.

"Hurry," Billy said, standing. "We've got to..."

Rustling.

Movement.

Over to his left.

He looked around.

Squinted into the darkness.

"Did you hear that?" Billy asked.

"I didn't hear anything," Marco said. "Come on. Quit stalling. Gotta get out of here."

But as Marco started to run again, Billy heard the movement again.

There was somebody here.

Definitely somebody here.

"Marco, I don't... I don't think we're alone."

Marco stopped. Slowed down. Then he walked back over to Billy. "The fuck you talking about?"

"There's someone over there. I can hear them."

"Well I don't hear a thing. And the sooner we get out of this place, the better. So come on. Let's…"

Movement.

And then something else.

Sobbing.

Crying?

Billy stood there, heart racing. If there was someone alive in here, someone like Sophie, then they could help them. Get them out of this place.

They couldn't just leave whoever it was behind.

He lifted his rifle.

And then, suddenly, an idea sparked in his mind.

"Torches," Billy said.

"Huh?"

"The rifles. They have… they have torches."

He reached for the top of the rifle. Searched for a switch.

And then he found it.

Put his finger against it.

Looked at Marco, who stood there, shaking his head in the darkness.

But pointing his rifle, too.

Pointing it at the movement.

Pointing it at the sobbing.

"Are you ready?" Billy asked.

Marco nodded. "Ready as I'll ever be."

Billy took a deep breath.

Swallowed a lump in his throat.

And then he flicked the switch.

When he saw who was sitting there in front of him, he almost fell over again.

CHAPTER TWENTY-FIVE

"Faye?" Billy said.

She was sitting right there in front of him in the darkness. Staring into space. Shivering. Snot dangled down from the bottom of her chin in a long, wobbly blob. Her cheeks were completely drenched with tears.

And her eyes were bloodshot and red.

So red.

Billy held his rifle. Pointed the light at Faye. Anger built up inside him. Anger towards Faye. Because if what Meg told him really was true... if Marco really had seen Faye leaving Jorah's place the night of the murder... then Faye was responsible for everything that had happened at Eastbrook.

It meant she was a traitor.

But as Billy stood there and watched her sob away to herself, he felt pity towards her.

Because he didn't *know* she was responsible.

He didn't *know* if that was true.

Not until he heard the words from Faye's lips herself.

But the way she was sitting here in the middle of this dark underpass.

An underpass filled with bodies.

Children's bodies.

As she sat here, Billy couldn't shake the feeling that she was responsible.

That she had played a part in the slaughter here.

That some of this was on her.

And that absolutely fucking terrified him.

Because he thought he knew Faye.

He thought he fucking *loved* Faye.

"What... what are you doing down here?" Billy asked.

Faye didn't say a word. She just kept on crying away. Shaking her head. Gasping for breath.

Billy took a step towards her. "Faye. We need... we need to get out of here."

Faye shook her head.

Drool fell from her chin, and foam formed in the corners of her mouth.

She looked... gone.

Completely gone.

Dead behind the eyes.

Billy stared with his torch shining right at her. And as she stared back at him, he knew. She didn't have to say a word. He could see it in her eyes. He could see it from the pain in her cries.

He knew guilt when he saw it.

He felt like he'd been punched in the gut. Tasted a bitter tang of vomit in his mouth. He felt dizzy. Started to sway from side to side a little.

Because Faye.

Not Faye.

Not the Faye he knew.

There was only one question he could ask that made any sense.

"Why?"

Faye looked up at him then. Right into his eyes. There was a lucidity to her gaze now. A clarity.

Her bottom lip turned. "I'm sorry. I'm so… He never promised me this. He promised me paradise. He—he promised paradise for you too."

Billy frowned. What the fuck was she talking about? Promised her paradise? And promised him paradise, too?

"I made—I made him promise to spare you. Not to kill you. So—so you could join me. So you'd be okay."

It clicked into place, then. She'd asked these bastards to spare his life. And that's why he was still standing. There was nothing special about him. They really were just people who kept their promises.

Fuck. This was messed up. This was so, so fucking messed up.

He shook his head. "Whoever made you these promises murdered our people, Faye. They murdered our children. They murdered… they murdered Steve."

Faye shook her head. Buried her head into her hands and let out a wail, which echoed through the dark tunnels. The sort of wail a mother made when they found out their child was dead.

And it made Billy feel sick. Not with pity. Not anymore.

Because he didn't feel pity towards Faye.

He just felt sadness.

He just felt betrayal.

Total betrayal.

He walked over to her.

"Billy?" Sophie asked.

But he didn't register her voice.

He just held his rifle in both hands now and pointed it at Faye.

"Billy?" Faye said. "What are you doing?"

Billy pressed the rifle to the top of Faye's head.

A lump swelled in his throat.

Anger rattled through his system.

"You sold us out. You… you stitched me up for Jorah's murder.

And then you had me locked away so you could help your new friends."

Faye shook her head. "I never knew it would be like this."

"I don't give a fuck *what* you thought it'd be like. This is how it is. Look around you."

"I don't—I don't want to—"

"Look around you!" Billy shouted.

"I can't!" Faye screamed.

She lifted her head. Snarled at Billy. Tears dripped from her cheeks.

"I see... I see it enough," she said. Burying her head in her hands again. "I see it all the time. I see it all the time!"

She started to scratch her eyes.

Dug her fingernails right into her skin and dragged it up and down, up and down, so hard it had to be doing some damage.

Billy wanted to step in. He wanted to stop her.

Because he used to admire this woman.

He used to have a major crush on her.

And for a time, he wondered if maybe, just maybe, she might be the one.

But watching her tear herself apart right now after causing all the horror she'd caused... Billy didn't feel anything towards her but hatred.

He heard something, then. A bang right up the top end of the underpass. A sudden glow of light.

Billy turned around.

The Liberators were here.

Shining their torches down towards him.

Running his way.

Billy's stomach sank. He knew there was no time to waste. He had to get away. Had to get Sophie away from this place.

Faye scratched her eyes. She banged her head back against the wall, again and again.

"Kill me," she said. "Kill... kill me. Please."

Billy's skin crawled. He shook his head. "I..."

"Come on, Billy," Marco said. "We need to get the hell out of here. Don't make me ditch you again."

Footsteps echoing through the underpass.

Faye banging her head against the wall.

"Kill me kill me kill me kill me..."

Billy tightened his finger on the trigger.

And then he let go.

He lowered the rifle.

"You don't get the easy way out for what you've done," Billy said.

Faye's bulging red eyes widened with horror. "Wh—what?"

"I've had enough trauma to deal with in my life. I don't need your death on my hands. Good luck with your new friends. You'll need it."

"No," Faye said. "No!"

Billy wasn't waiting around any longer.

He grabbed Sophie's hand.

"Come on," he said. "Time to go."

And then he ran as fast as he could, up the underpass, and into the darkness.

Behind, he swore he heard Faye scream.

CHAPTER TWENTY-SIX

Billy looked back at Eastbrook, and he knew he was at the final hurdle now.

He was just outside the community gates. It was still light above ground. Felt like the longest day ever. He had no sense at all what time of day it was or even what day it was. None of that mattered right now.

It was Eastbrook's last day. That's how he would remember it.

Didn't matter how much he tried to run from it. How much he tried to hide from it. How much he tried to resist it.

He would always remember today as the day his community fell.

Rain sprinkled down from the grey clouds above. A breeze picked up, carrying the smell of smoke through the streets. He could taste blood on his dry, cracked lips. Sweat. Vomit. He couldn't stop shivering. Couldn't stop shaking.

Just kept thinking of the people he'd lost.

People like Steve.

And even people like Faye.

It was Faye's betrayal that really stung him right now. The thought that she would sell him out. And was what she'd told him true? Was the reason they were keeping him alive as simple as Faye asking them to?

And if they had...

Fuck, that was a guilt he had to live with. A guilt of still being alive.

Because he shouldn't still be alive.

He should be dead right now.

He should be dead like everyone else.

But instead, he was alive with the horrifying knowledge that everyone else was gone.

He stood there with Sophie's warm hand in his, and he remembered something.

Not *everyone* was gone.

He looked down at her. Standing there, blonde hair trailing down her shoulders. Grey-faced and pale. Eyes wide. Not smiling but looking traumatised.

He knew trauma. He knew what it felt like to have no hope as a kid.

But there was hope.

As much as it seemed distant sometimes... there really was hope out there.

And he needed to make sure Sophie knew that.

He felt Rex licking his ear then. A big slobbery tongue sticking inside his ear, licking away, nibbling at him.

And even though his breath stunk, and his saliva was so fucking thick and gooey... Billy was just glad he was still here. Glad he was still alive.

Barely. Fuck, Billy wasn't even sure if he'd walk again.

But hell, what did it matter?

He'd carry him on his back to the edge of the earth if he had to.

He looked at Marco, then. Not the ally he expected. Standing there, rifle in hand. Haunted expression on his face. Behind, he knew they were running out of time. That the Liberators would be here soon. So they had to take this opportunity and get out of Eastbrook while they could.

But still, it just felt... wrong.

"I feel like I'm betraying everyone," Billy said. "I feel like... like I'm betraying *him*."

Billy didn't have to tell Marco who he meant for him to know he meant Steve.

And something Billy kind of appreciated about Marco right now?

Something he respected?

Marco didn't try to beat around the bush and tell Billy what he wanted to hear.

He just nodded. "It's shit. It's fucking bullshit. I want to stay here. I want to fight. I want to murder every one of these fuckers. But... but you know damn well as I do that ain't happening. Not like this."

Billy looked out at the streets. He looked at the smoke rising in the distance. He looked at the bodies lying still, face down in a pool of their own blood. He saw smashed windows of homes that were so peaceful before today. And it made him angry. It made him furious. Because it was wrong. It was so, so wrong.

And then he took a deep breath of that warm, humid air, and he let it go.

Because yes, he'd made a promise to Steve.

A promise to fight for this community.

A promise to fight for *everyone*.

But there was only one way he was fighting for Eastbrook.

For everyone.

And that was by getting away from here.

He crouched down. Looked into Sophie's bright blue eyes. Wiped a tear from her cheek. "We'll be okay. We'll get you out of here, and we'll get somewhere safe. I promise."

She stared into Billy's eyes. Opened her mouth like she was

going to say something. And then she just nodded and smiled a little. "I know we will."

Billy felt a warmth inside his chest. Seeing that this kid trusted him to get her out of here counted for a hell of a lot.

He just had to deliver on that fucking promise, that was for sure.

He stood back up, Rex's weight pushing down on his shoulders.

He looked over at Eastbrook. Over at the buildings that used to house such life. The streets that were filled with such laughter. A place he was proud to call home for so, so many years.

And he looked over towards where he knew Steve lived.

Thought about the beers in the garden they used to share.

The laughs they'd have listening to Steve attempt to play his guitar and snapping two strings going too hard on Wonderwall.

The arguments they'd had about totally irrelevant shit like what went in the bins and what went in recycling; shit that seemed so important at the time, but shit that didn't matter, not in the grand scheme of things.

He even missed those arguments.

He swallowed a lump in his throat. "I'll do you proud, Dad. I promise."

He tightened his grip on Sophie's hand.

He turned around.

And together, with Marco and Sophie by his side, and Rex on his shoulders, he walked.

CHAPTER TWENTY-SEVEN

General Watts looked out over the community called Eastbrook and felt really proud of the work they'd done here today.

It was getting dark. Late afternoon. It'd been a long day. A long day marching through the streets. A long day dragging people out of their homes.

A long day putting a bullet into the skulls of every one of these survivors.

He didn't feel any guilt over what he was doing. Because it was what he *had* to do. It was all in the name of unity. In centrality.

It was all in the name of clearing the canvas so his people could develop and mould the world into one *they* wanted.

The warring, independent little factions of the world over the last decade or so had been too destructive. They'd dragged things back to the dark ages.

And if General Watts had learned one thing from the last decade, it was that people wouldn't willingly kneel. Ever.

Sure, they might *pretend* they're kneeling, and they might even follow orders and stand in line for a good while, too.

But it never lasted.

These people had grown too used to being free.

They'd grown too set in their ways.

It was the job of people like General Watts to bring order back to them—and to bring order back to the whole country.

He looked around the streets before him. He looked at the piles of dead bodies, burning now. He smelled the charred flesh. Tasted it in the air. A tickle in his throat with that smoke. His asthma flaring up again.

He remembered what Mum used to tell him about his asthma. How it made him different to the other kids. How it meant he couldn't learn to cycle and couldn't go roller skating or swimming. How he shouldn't even go to the park at night for too long because he had to be back home with her, looking after her.

He remembered all these things and felt tension in his gut.

Then he looked around, and he smiled.

He'd come a long way since then.

He looked around, and he saw his people. All lined up before him. Rifles in hand. Staring at him as they stood there in their perfect grey. Following him. Devoted to him. Completely and utterly devoted to him.

He knew these people would do anything for him. They would do anything for their cause. They would die for their cause. Because they truly believed in their cause. And they truly believed in the leader of their cause, too.

Not just him. He *was* their leader, of course.

But there was somebody above even him.

Everybody took orders from somebody.

But he took orders from the highest.

He looked around at them all standing there. Still. Totally still. He could drop a pin, and he'd hear it from a mile away.

Broken glass all over the ground.

Smashed up windows.

Blood.

Bodies.

Death.

Destruction.

He looked at it all, and for a moment, for just a moment, he felt sad. He felt regret. He felt dread.

Because these were people too.

But then he knew what they were.

And he knew what they were capable of.

He knew the pain they'd caused over years, centuries, millennia.

And he knew it was his cause that had the opportunity to wipe the slate totally clean.

To make Britain truly united, from top to bottom, once again.

He looked around to his left, and he saw the woman called Faye kneeling there, sobbing.

He felt a glimmer of disgust in his chest when he looked at her. She was the one who'd helped him in. She was the one who he'd made so many promises to.

And her only wish?

The one person she wanted saving?

Billy.

He looked at her, and he felt pity and disgust, and he wished he wasn't a man of his word.

Because he hated these filthy animals.

He hated the lot of them.

He wanted them all dead.

But... a promise *was* a promise.

And besides. The women were useful.

Very useful.

Not only useful but they were required.

Especially the attractive ones.

He stroked Faye's sweaty hair from her forehead, and he turned around and saw more women up ahead.

On their knees.

Tape around their mouths.

And a few younger ones, too.

Teenagers.

Perfect and pristine and ready.

He looked at the bodies, and he knew it was sad that they'd had to waste so many good ones.

But that was just a part of the process.

They didn't need many. Only a few. The best few.

The rest were all part of the fear.

The rest were all part of the chaos.

The rest were all part of the destruction.

He looked to his right, then. And he saw Tristan kneeling there. Eyes blackened and bruised. Staring up, just like the rest of his people. Proud but defiant.

He knew Tristan had turned on his people. He'd seen it himself. Helping that sewer rat, Billy, escape. And slaughtering his own.

He gritted his teeth, and he stood there, rifle in hand.

"You know what happens to traitors," Watts said. "You all know what happens to traitors."

He looked around at his people.

Still.

Unmoving.

Then he looked back at Tristan, who knelt before him.

Who stared up into his eyes.

"At least I know I did the right thing," he gasped. "At least... at least for once in my life, I know I did the right thing."

General Watts laughed. Smiled. "I won't make a martyr of you."

And then he cracked him over the skull with the butt of his rifle.

Sent him collapsing to the ground, twitching, saliva frothing at the corners of his lips.

He looked around at his people. So loyal. So trusting. "Get the streets cleared. And get the women back to base for processing. It's time for us to rest. And then... it's time for us to begin our next phase."

CHAPTER TWENTY-EIGHT

Billy opened his eyes and felt a bolt of fear in his chest the second he heard the bang outside.

It was dark. Pitch black. And he felt cold. Really cold. Summer suddenly felt like a long time ago. Three months had passed since the escape from Eastbrook, and in a way, it still felt like yesterday.

The shock felt just as raw.

The memories felt just as vivid.

The smell of smoke.

The bright red blood.

And the cold bodies on the ground all around, totally still.

Billy felt his stomach turn as he sat upright. He was on a rickety bed he called his own. Springs shooting up through the mattress. A smell of old cigarette smoke filled the room.

But it was enough. It would do. It was a roof over his head.

And when the Liberators were out there, and their numbers seemed to be increasing rapidly by the day... yeah, you kind of had to take everything as it came.

He looked around, over at the cobweb-covered window. Bright moonlight shone in through the cracks. He could feel a draft creeping into the room, rattling against the window. Even though he was freezing, he was covered in sweat.

He'd been dreaming again.

The nightmares weren't the ones he used to have anymore. Not being locked away in a dark room, tied up, trapped. It seemed like he'd exorcised that demon.

His dreams now were of Steve.

Steve and Faye and Tristan.

All of them swimming around in an intensely hot furnace of lava.

Grabbing the melted rock on the sides of the pit and trying to heave themselves up out of there.

Looking up at him with burned faces, skin dangling from the bone, and tears of blood pouring down their cheeks and screaming: "Why? Why? Why?"

He heard that chant echoing in his skull, and then he heard footsteps downstairs.

He climbed out of bed. Slowly. There was someone in the house. It wasn't Marco. Marco slept like a log and didn't snore even slightly, something he liked to boast about. And Sophie... Sophie was far too afraid to leave her bedroom after dark. He'd tried to convince her not to be afraid of the dark. That he used to be scared of it too, but that it really wasn't anything to worry about.

But in a way, Billy was kind of grateful for Sophie's reluctance about the dark. It meant she wouldn't go wandering at night.

And it also meant that unless Rex had suddenly rediscovered the ability to walk again, the old lump, then there was definitely someone downstairs right now.

He walked across the bedroom, being careful not to creak any floorboards—which was tricky in an old place filled with creaky fucking floorboards. He tried to listen out for any more sounds, but all he could hear was ringing in his ears. That damp smell that always hit him when he woke up hit him with full force once again. And that sickening, gut-wrenching feeling in the pit of his stomach, which came with the territory of having spent the last three months fleeing the Liberators and then searching for their Ulston home Tristan told them about and finding nothing, and basically spending life on the road counting down the days until the apocalypse engulfed them completely.

But as he stood there in the darkness, he knew he had bigger, more immediate problems on his hands right now.

And that was the person downstairs.

He walked across his bedroom. Over to the bedroom door. He saw movement in the corners of his eyes. Shadows, taking on human form, threatening to creep out and pull him into them.

He just focused ahead. He couldn't get distracted. He had to find out who the hell was in his home, and then he had to deal the fuck with them.

He glanced out the window.

Moonlight shone down onto the empty streets outside.

Three cars in the road, overturned, covered in weeds.

A bin lid rattling in the wind like it always did.

No sign of any Liberators.

That was something.

He walked over to the bedroom door. Grabbed the rifle he'd stolen from the Liberators. He stood by the bedroom door, part of him not wanting to step outside, part of him knowing he didn't want to come across whatever he was going to come across.

But knowing he had no choice.

He opened the door.

Stepped out onto the dark, dusty hallway.

Walked across more of the floorboards towards the top of the stairs.

He thought about giving Marco and Sophie the heads up. But he didn't want to alarm Sophie. And besides. He didn't want to waste any time. He had to get on with this. Fast.

He walked over to the top of the stairs when he saw something move.

He froze.

There was someone down there.

There was somebody in the lounge.

He crept down the stairs. Rifle raised. Heart racing. Shaking a little. And he knew he was insane. He knew he should just give Marco a heads up. He knew he shouldn't go wandering down here on his own.

But here he was.

Halfway down the stairs.

Rifle raised.

Ready to fire at whoever crossed his path.

He reached the bottom step.

Looked around in the open-plan lounge/dining area of this old, detached house.

Squinted into the furthest corners of the lounge.

And then into the kitchen area.

He looked across the room towards where he'd seen that movement when he heard something rattling.

A pan, by the sounds of things.

A pan hitting the floor.

Billy held his breath.

His heart raced.

He walked over the wooden floor.

Slowly.

Rifle raised.

Shaking in his hands.

"Who's—who's there?" he said.

No response.

Silence.

He walked further across the wooden floor.

Right over to where he'd seen that movement.

And he saw a dark mound on the floor beneath him.

The hairs on the back of his neck stood on end.

He went to pull the trigger.

"I wouldn't if I were you."

He jumped out of his skin.

Swung around.

Went to fire at that voice.

That woman's voice.

That... familiar voice.

"Don't shoot, Billy. Not a good idea at all."

"Who the fuck are you?"

The woman laughed. "Surely you haven't forgotten me already."

Billy's heart raced.

He pointed the rifle at the dark silhouette standing opposite him, enshrouded in moonlight.

He flicked the torch on so it shone into this woman's eyes.

The woman lifted a hand. Covered her face. "Shit. You got no manners these days or something?"

But as Billy stood there, shaking, he realised he knew exactly who this was.

"Meg," he said.

Meg squinted into the light, and she smiled. "Hello, stranger. Now can you put the fucking gun down and get that light out of my eyes? We've a hell of a lot to catch up on."

CHAPTER TWENTY-NINE

"What the fuck do you think you're fucking doing?" Billy shouted.

"Me? I'm not the one pointing a fucking gun at you. What the fuck do you think *you're* doing?"

"You're—you're in my home."

"It's not your home. Technically."

"You're in my home in the middle of the fucking night. What the fuck do you expect?"

Meg lifted a hand and waved Billy off. "Look. You know who it is now. I'm sorry for the scare. Is that what you want to hear? Okay. I'm very sorry for scaring you. There. Happy now?"

Billy shook his head as he stood there in the darkness of this downstairs space. Moonlight shone through the window opposite, illuminating Meg, who stood before him.

Meg, who he hadn't seen since the day Eastbrook fell.

The day he was captured.

The day everything went to shit.

Meg, who did a runner when it suited—and then left Billy and the rest of his people to...

Well. To *die*.

Billy kept his rifle pointed at her. "Nice of you to show up after all these months. Been keeping well?"

"I've been better. But it is nice to see you, I will admit."

"Don't give me that bullshit. My people died. My entire home was destroyed."

"Just as I warned you it would be. And if it weren't for my warning… you'd be dead, too. So maybe you should count your blessings rather than shooting the messenger."

Billy stepped forward. Pushed a rifle right to Meg's chest. "You have some nerve coming in here."

"So you keep telling me," Meg said.

Billy heard footsteps then. Upstairs. Marco. Racing out of his room, clumsily tumbling down the staircase. "Billy? What the hell's going on?"

Meg raised an eyebrow as she squinted into his torchlight. "Company? Not exactly what I expected.

Marco lifted his rifle and pointed it at her. "Who the hell is… Wait. I recognise her."

"Surprise," Meg said, waving her hands.

"What the hell is she doing here?" Marco asked.

"Jeez," Meg said. "What is it with you people and your welcomes tonight?"

"You could've fucking knocked," Billy said. "You could've got yourself shot."

Meg shrugged. And then she lifted an apple out of nowhere, crunched it. "I dunno. I guess this way was more exciting."

Billy shook his head. "You're insane."

"Maybe so," Meg said. "But I'm here. So, are you going to show me around your lovely little home? Or are you going to stand there pointing your guns at me? Or get on with shooting me?"

Meg walked around the room. She scraped her finger across the top of the dusty leather sofa before putting her finger to her lips. She looked around at the chipped walls and the old paintings, completely covered in dust. "Nice place you've got here," she said. "I like what you've done with it. Gone for the real shithole vibe, I see."

"What the fuck are you doing here?" Billy asked.

Meg turned around. Smiled. "You're a curious customer, aren't you?" And then she took a big crunch of her apple and sighed. "That's the big question, isn't it?"

"And it's a question you'd better answer fast if you want to keep your head on your shoulders."

"Billy?"

A voice.

A voice over by the stairs.

Sophie.

Billy's stomach sank. He didn't like Sophie witnessing violence. She'd seen enough in her short life already.

He forced a smile at her and tried to look calm. Well. As calm as a man pointing a rifle at a woman in the middle of the night could possibly be, anyway. "It's... it's okay, Sophie. You go back to bed."

Sophie held on to the stair rails and stared through the gap at Meg. "Who... who is she?"

Meg turned around, started walking towards her. "Hello, Little Miss. Who would you be?"

"I wouldn't move another fucking muscle if you want to live," Billy shouted.

Meg stopped. She looked around at him. Narrowed her eyes and smirked like she thought he was calling her bluff.

But she stayed put. Which meant he'd got his message across well enough, at least.

"Look," Meg said, pacing back towards the sofa. "While you two have been fannying around, I've actually been doing some research."

"What sort of research?"

"Research that you might want to learn about."

"It better be good, whatever it is."

Meg smiled again. "Oh, it's good."

She walked around the sofa. Sat herself down on it. Stretched out her legs, threw her apple core into the old fireplace, and then stretched out her arms and lay back on them.

"But... y'know, it is late."

"What?"

"I mean, I might just kick my shoes off, and we can talk about this in the morning. You seemed pretty moody about being woken up. Is he always like this?"

Billy wasn't taking any of this shit anymore.

He rushed over to the sofa.

He grabbed Meg by the scruff of her neck.

Dragged her towards him.

"Listen," he said. "I don't give a fuck what you think. I don't give a shit about you saving me before. And frankly, as much as I'm sorry for the things you've lost, boo fucking hoo. We've all been there."

Meg's eyes widened. Clearly, that one stung.

"But I'm not playing your fucking games. You come in here in the middle of the night after three fucking months. Acting like you're on fucking crack. You tell me. You look me in the eyes, and you tell me why you're here now. Or I'll have no qualms putting a bullet in your head. I am deadly fucking serious."

She looked back at him. Her eyes scanned his face for some kind of sign he might be joking. Judging from the seriousness of her expression, she didn't find any. "Okay," she said. "Okay. But can you just... can you just let go of me, please?"

Billy tightened his grip.

Then he pushed her back onto the sofa.

"Talk," he said.

She looked around at Marco and Sophie. Then back at Billy. "Jesus. You've changed—"

Billy lifted his rifle. "I watched my people die. I've spent the last three months trying to figure out how to avenge them. How to destroy these fuckers. But I've got nowhere. All I've been able to do is run from them. Don't talk to me about changing. Don't you dare say a thing about it."

"Hey," Meg said. "I didn't say you'd changed for the worst."

"She has a point," Marco said.

Billy shot daggers at him with his eyes.

Marco lowered his head. "Sorry."

Billy looked back at Meg then.

She sat there, looking right up at him. That happy act she carried around with her earlier seemed to have gone. That confidence, that swagger, faded.

"Talk to me," Billy said. "Tell me why you're here. And tell me why you're so fucking smug."

She looked up at him, and she smiled.

"I'm here because I have good news," she said. "Very, very good news."

Billy narrowed his eyes. "Go on."

"Why don't you sit down?" Meg said. "You might need it. With what I'm about to tell you."

"I don't need to sit down."

Meg's eyes widened. "You don't?"

"No."

"And you're absolutely sure about that?"

"Just get the fuck on with the story, okay?"

Meg smiled. "Okay," she said. "But don't say I didn't warn you."

And then she told Billy everything.

CHAPTER THIRTY

Billy stood in the middle of the darkness of his lounge and tried to wrap his head around what Meg just told him.

He couldn't hear anything anymore. He thought Marco might be saying something, asking questions, but he wasn't sure. He felt dizzy. His head was spinning, and he felt sick.

Not sick with nerves, though.

Not sick with the kind of dread he usually felt.

But sick with excitement.

Sick with adrenaline?

He looked at Meg sitting there on his sofa in the light of his rifle, and he couldn't think what to say.

What to ask her.

So, in the end, he could only ask one question.

One stupid ass question.

"What?" he asked.

Meg smiled a little wider. "I told you you'd be better taking a seat."

"Just... just tell me what you told me again. But without the bullshit this time."

Meg opened her mouth to say something. Then closed it.

Sighed. "There's a place. Around ten miles from here. Fulton, it calls itself."

"I got that part. But the next part."

"The part about it having power?"

Billy nodded.

"The part about the tall walls? The part about the armed guards lining those walls? And the part about this place being a sanctuary for people? Away from the outside world? Away from the Liberators? That part?"

Billy heard Meg say these words, and he couldn't take it all in.

He couldn't believe it.

A place with power?

That was far-fetched enough. But he knew there were places like that once upon a time. Aoife used to live somewhere with electricity. Somewhere run by some old government who tried getting things back on track many years ago.

But that was a long time ago. Those days were long gone. They were dead.

Now?

Today?

"Bullshit," Billy said.

"I thought you might say that," Meg said. "And I don't blame you. If someone told me the same thing, I don't think I'd be too keen on believing them."

Billy's heart raced. His chest tightened. He couldn't think. Didn't know what the fuck to say.

Just kept on getting dizzier and dizzier…

"Who—who run this place? If it's—if it's for real."

"That's the catch," Meg said. "I don't actually know."

Marco sighed. "Great. Well this plan's a damned non-starter."

"But I know they are good people."

"And how do you know that?" Billy asked.

"I saw kids there. I saw… I saw families there. These people. They're not like the Liberators. They're—they're different."

Billy shook his head. "I don't like it."

"What's not to like?" Meg asked.

"You've changed your tune."

"Huh?"

"When I last saw you, you were telling me the only hope in the wake of the Liberators was by warning enough communities before they got pulverised by them. Building some sort of... some sort of greater community to step up and destroy them. And now you're talking about just sulking away to some paradise where everything's good? What does that mean for everyone else?"

Meg stood, then. She walked over to Billy. Stood right in front of him. "Look. I... I know how it sounds. You've got to remember I've lost someone too. My boy. My Noah. And my people. Just like you have."

Billy nodded. "I know that. Which makes it hard for me to understand why you're giving up the fight."

"I'm not giving up any fight," Meg said. "I've just... I've realised I'll never get what I want. Not just logistically. Like, let's say by chance I manage to get to the Liberators, and I get to destroy the whole fucking lot of them, which isn't gonna happen. Even then... it won't bring Noah back."

"But it might save other communities—"

"It's too late for the other communities," she said.

Hearing those words, hearing the defeat in Meg's voice, made Billy's stomach sink. Because this woman used to be filled with such hope for defeating the Liberators. For standing together and saving more communities.

Her entire goals had changed.

And the worst thing?

Billy knew she was right.

"I'm not... I'm not giving up. Maybe these people will help us achieve what we want to achieve. But even if they don't... it's time we started thinking about ourselves. We've survived. Whether we like it or not, no matter how guilty we are about it... we're here.

And we have a chance. A chance to get to someplace nicer than what we have. And a chance to help people like… like that kiddo over there have something of a normal life. For as long as that lasts."

Billy looked over at Sophie. She stood there on the stairs, staring through the rails, right into his eyes. She looked so innocent. And so lost. And there was nothing he wanted more than to get her to safety. To get her to a new home.

But his own battle?

His promise to help stand up against these Liberators?

To ultimately destroy them?

The promise he'd made to Steve to fight for his people?

But then… his people were right here, weren't they?

And who else was he fighting for but them?

"I know it's not an easy choice to make," Meg said. "And if you're not in, I'll walk right out this door right now, and I'll make my own way there. But I just… Well. I found you. After all these years, I found you. That sort of luck just doesn't happen. Especially not in this world."

Billy looked across at Marco, who looked right back at Billy.

"What do you think?" Billy asked.

Marco took a deep breath. Sighed. "I think… I think it sounds good. Maybe too good to be true. But I don't see what other choices we have. We've been on the road for three months now. Things ain't getting better for us. Doesn't… doesn't Sophie deserve better at this point?"

Billy nodded.

He looked back at Meg.

"Sleep on it. Think about it if you need to. There's no great rush. Well. Only a death cult sweeping across the country and destroying everything in its path. But hell, you've made it this far, haven't you?"

Billy swallowed a lump in his throat.

He clenched his fists together.

And he forced a smile.

"I don't think we need to sleep on it," he said.

Meg frowned. "Huh?"

"We've spent long enough on the road. We've spent long enough convincing ourselves we can destroy them. That we can fight them. But some battles can't be won."

Marco nodded.

"I... I made a promise. A promise to someone very close to me. I promised I'd fight for my people. I didn't know what it meant at the time. Not exactly. Or at least I thought I knew what it meant. But now I see I didn't know what it meant at all."

"And what does it mean?" Meg said.

Billy glanced at Sophie again, and he smiled.

Then, he looked Meg right in the eye. "We're going to join you. We're going to go to this Fulton place. And... and we're going to start a new home there."

CHAPTER THIRTY-ONE

Billy looked out of the window into the morning light, and for the first time in a long time, he knew exactly where he had to go and what he had to do.

It was snowing. Big flakes fell from above, coating the frozen ground. It looked a pretty day out there. Quiet. Still. Peaceful. He could hear the birds singing in the trees. Smell the fresh air wafting in through the cracks in the window. And he could taste the roasted squirrel on his lips. A breakfast he hoped would last a while.

Because today was the first day of their journey.

Their final journey?

He wasn't sure. But it was beginning to feel that way.

He heard a whine behind him, and he smiled. Rex was back on his shoulders again. The old lump *still* couldn't walk. Either that, or he was just growing lazier and lazier by the day, and he'd kind of got used to being carted around everywhere.

Marco rolled his eyes. Told Billy they should leave him behind. That it'd be the kindest thing.

Billy told him there was more chance he'd leave Marco behind than his dog.

He looked out and saw Marco and Meg out there, talking to one another about something. They seemed to be getting along, weirdly. Strange, considering the last time the pair had met, Marco pointed a gun at her.

But then Billy never used to be the biggest fan of Marco either. So he figured it wasn't too much of a surprise.

Especially with how unpredictable and eccentric Meg seemed.

Hell. There were no such things as surprises in this world. Not anymore.

Footsteps creaked down the stairs behind Billy.

He turned around.

Sophie walked towards him. Her head was lowered. She held on to a little pink rucksack. Avoided eye contact with Billy.

"Hey," he said. "You ready?"

Sophie nodded at him. Didn't say a word.

She'd been like this all morning, ever since Meg got here, actually. At first, Billy put it down to tiredness and maybe a few nerves about the sudden change in circumstances.

But he was beginning to wonder if something else might be going on here.

"If you want to talk about anything," Billy said. "I know... I know it can be helpful. To get things off your chest."

She glanced up at him.

Then looked away again.

Billy sighed. "Sophie. I know... I know it's scary. And I know it's always scary when things are about to change. Or when we have to go on another journey. But things will be better when we get to this Fulton place. I promise. Things will be much better than they've ever been."

"It's not that."

Wow. First time she'd spoken. That was something, at least. "Then what is it?"

She glanced up at him again. And this time, she sighed. "I just... When we get there. What if people there don't like us?"

"It's... it's something I've thought about," Billy said. "But we can't let that stop us from trying."

"And what if they do like us, and—and then the Liberators come and—"

"Sophie," Billy said. Calmly but firmly. He thought about lying. About promising her the Liberators would never appear again. That they were long gone now. Far behind them. And that, based on the things Meg had told them, this new place was safe from them anyway.

But at the same time... Billy didn't want to lie.

"Look," he said. "I don't know what we're going to find. I don't know whether we'll be welcomed. And even if we are, I don't know that we'll still be there in a year. And it's rubbish. It really is rubbish. But... but the only other option is floating along like this. No goal in mind. No hope in sight. And I don't want to live that way."

Sophie stared into his eyes. Wordless.

"I made Steve a promise. That I'd fight for my people. And this is fighting for my people."

"So when we get there, you aren't going to try fighting them again?"

That question shocked Billy a little. Came out of nowhere. He looked away. "No."

"You're lying."

Shit. She was sharp. Or he was being too obvious. Either way, it wasn't good.

He looked back at her. "I can't just let them go on doing what they're doing. Slaughtering people. People like us. Kids like... like you."

"But what are you going to do? How are you going to stop them?"

Billy remembered what Tristan told him. Ulston. The place where he could "weaken" them somehow. The time he'd spent searching for that place, with no positive outcome.

And then he thought about all the other communities around the country that would still be standing, large and small. If they could all pool their resources together, then maybe, just maybe, they could fight back.

He knew it was a long shot. But he couldn't just give up.

He walked over to Sophie.

He held out a hand.

"Whatever happens, I'm here with you. Okay? Whatever happens, we're going to get to this new place. We're going to check it out. And if it's good, great. And if it's not, well... the last few months have been alright really, haven't they?"

Sophie smiled at him. "Yeah. They have."

He felt a warmth in his chest. Smiled back at her. "Now come on. Let's get going. One thing you'll soon learn about snow is, as pretty as it is, it's a fucking nightmare to travel in."

"My mum used to tell me it was hard to drive in. And I imagined... I imagined it would be thicker. And gooey. But now... now it looks nice. It looks like the nicest thing I've ever seen."

She took Billy's hand.

They walked over to the door together.

Opened it and stepped out into the cold.

They stood there in the snow together. Flakes hitting Billy's face as it fell, so quiet, so peaceful.

He looked down at Sophie, and he saw she was crying.

"You okay?" he asked.

She sniffed. "It's just... it's just so beautiful."

Billy looked up at the sky. At the trees, dusted in white. "Yeah," he said. "Yeah, it is."

He tightened his grip on Sophie's hand.

She tightened back.

And then, together, they walked.

Into the beautiful snow.

One final push.

CHAPTER THIRTY-TWO

She peeked through the trees at the people leaving the cabin, and a smile crept up her face.

It was snowing. She loved the snow. Always so pretty, like a fairy-tale. It reminded her of being a little girl. One of her earliest memories. Sitting there in her cot and staring up at these white balls falling from the sky, while behind her somewhere, Mum and Dad screamed at one another.

She watched those white balls falling from the sky and didn't even notice Mum's scream.

She didn't even notice Dad run past her, blood on his hands.

Knife in his hand.

She didn't notice at the time, but she remembered that moment well now.

Very, very well.

The air was cold. Biting cold. Colder than Maria felt in quite some time. The last time it was anywhere near this cold, she'd lost two toes and a finger.

She really thought she'd miss them at the time. But she soon learned to adapt.

That was just the way of the world now, wasn't it?

Adapt or die.

That's how it was now. And in a way, it's how it'd always been.

She saw the figures moving through the woods. The man, with the dog on his back, something Maria found quite amusing really. Bless him. Humanity's attachment to animals. And humanity's attachment to the weak. The need to prop others up in times of need.

It was sweet.

But it was also a handicap.

A handicap this species had to move on from—fast—if it wanted to survive.

There were three others. A man, stockier than the one with the dog on his back. Holding one of these fancy rifles—the sort Maria really wouldn't mind getting her hands on.

A woman, too. Although she didn't have a rifle. She looked skinny. And more dishevelled than the others, somehow. Like she'd been out here in the wild a lot longer.

And then there was somebody else.

A little girl.

Blonde hair.

Blue eyes.

A little girl who reminded her of her Eve.

She thought about Eve, and she felt a knot in her stomach.

Eve's little laugh.

The warmth of her body when she cuddled up to her at night.

She looked at this little girl right now, and as she squinted at her, she really convinced herself she could be Eve.

She could tell herself she was Eve.

She could lie to herself...

A flash in her mind.

Memories.

Other little girls.

Other little Eves.

The other Eves who she'd rescued but just weren't good enough, just weren't—

She shook her head.

Took a deep breath.

She didn't have to think about those.

This was *her* Eve.

Her Eve and Simon's Eve.

Their beloved daughter, right here before them.

Simon was going to be so, so proud of her when he got back.

She swallowed a lump in her throat.

Tightened her grip on her knife.

And then she looked right at this little blonde girl, and she smiled.

It was time to get her Eve back.

CHAPTER THIRTY-THREE

Billy wasn't sure how long he'd been walking when he got that awful yet familiar feeling he was being watched.

The sky above was bright. Afternoon snow fell heavier than this morning. It was going to be a thick covering by the time it finished. Sophie seemed to be enjoying crunching her feet through it, savouring that satisfying crunching sound she'd never experienced before. Which was nice to witness. Nice to see.

The houses either side of them were covered in snow now. Some of them had rusty cars in their drives from years ago. It struck Billy that cars were pretty much just like trees now. Parts of the scenery. How weird they must be to kids born in the post-car world. Just as ever-present a part of the environment as plants.

A reminder of a world that once was.

Billy looked up at the windows of each of the houses. He just had a funny feeling someone was close. Couldn't explain it. Couldn't put his finger on it. But you know the feeling. That instinctive feeling that makes the hair on the back of your neck stand on end when you just know someone is there.

Watching.

Closely.

He listened to Marco and Meg's footsteps crunching through the snow. Felt Sophie's freezing cold hand, tight in his grip. He wasn't letting her go any time soon, that was for sure. He wasn't *ever* letting her go.

"I want to go play in it," Sophie said.

Billy looked down at her. Frowned. "What?"

"The snow," Sophie said. "Mum told me... Mum told me there were these things called snowmen. And I kind of wanted to build a snow-lady. Can I do that?"

Billy glanced up at Marco and Meg, who walked on. Rex continued his stellar contribution to the group of weighing down heavily on his shoulders, occasionally slavering on Billy's face, something he appreciated. "We... we kind of have to keep moving. We don't really have time to stop."

"Just—just a small one. Please. It won't take long. I just... I've never seen snow before. I want to make Mum. In snow."

Billy stood there, heart racing. Shit. She really had him over a barrel. He got it. Like, he *really* got it. The kid was a kid, and she should be allowed to be a kid.

But at the same time...

That feeling he had.

The feeling someone was watching.

The feeling someone was close.

"I promise it won't take long," Sophie said. "I just... Please. Can I?"

Billy looked around the street. It was pretty open in all truth. If anyone appeared, he'd have plenty of time to intervene before anything happened.

He looked at the tall trees at the backs of the gardens of these houses. Swaying in the breeze.

He took a deep breath, and he sighed. "Five minutes," he said.

Sophie's eyes lit up. "Really?"

"Five minutes, and that's it. No idea what you're gonna make in that time, but that's all you've got."

"Thank you," Sophie said. "Thank you."

She pulled away from him.

Tried to drag her hand from him.

He didn't want to let go.

Didn't want to let her loose.

But then he took a deep breath.

She'd be okay.

He had to trust her.

He let go.

Felt coldness where there was once warmth.

She walked. Just a few steps from him, over to the front garden of a semi-detached house with a Land Rover sitting in the front.

Knelt, delight on her face and in her eyes, and started working on her snow lady.

"I'll make it good," she said, smiling back at Billy. "I promise I'll make it good."

"Just make it quick," Billy said. "I won't be judging it on anything else..."

A shout.

A shout up the road.

Billy's stomach sank.

He swung around.

Rex growling on his shoulders.

Marco and Meg stood there in front of him.

Rifles raised.

"Billy!" Meg shouted. "Over here. Right now."

Billy gritted his teeth.

He looked around at Sophie, who was still working on her snow lady.

He didn't want to leave her.

But at the same time...

If there was trouble up ahead, he didn't want her to get involved.

He gritted his teeth.

"Don't you move a muscle," he said.

And then he ran up the road.

Over to Marco and Meg.

Marco stood there, rifle pointed ahead.

Meg by his side.

Rex's growling growing louder now.

"What?" Billy said. "What is…"

And then he saw it.

Lying there on the road.

Something that sent shivers up his spine.

Something that made his toes curl.

On the road before them, there was a girl.

A young girl. About Sophie's age.

Blonde, like Sophie.

Blue-eyed, like Sophie.

But there was one key difference with this kid and Sophie.

This kid was emaciated.

Her blonde hair was all patchy.

And she was dead.

"Liberators?" Marco said.

Meg stared at the road in front of them both. Shook her head. "I don't… I don't think so."

Billy felt fear inside.

This girl.

Her resemblance to Sophie.

They needed to get away from here.

Far, far away from here.

He turned around, expecting Sophie to be there, just up the road, waiting for him.

"Come on, Sophie," he started. "We've…"

And then he saw something that made his stomach sink to new depths.

Or rather, it was what he didn't see that made his stomach sink.

Sophie.

Sophie was gone.

CHAPTER THIRTY-FOUR

"Sophie!" Billy shouted.

Snow fell heavily from above. Other than the snow clouds, the afternoon skies were perfect blue. The pavements were covered in snow. Little prints where they'd walked along. The semi-detached houses either side of them stood over them, staring down at them like they were watching.

Everything was silent.

Silent, but for the breeze.

Silent, but for Billy's shout echoing down this street.

A sickening sensation in his stomach and his chest tightening its grip every second.

The taste of vomit building up in his dry mouth.

His head growing dizzy.

The smell of his own sweat getting stronger by the second.

The spot.

The spot right in front of the house where Billy left Sophie just moments earlier.

A little mound of snow on the garden.

And then, where Sophie was, nothing.

"Billy?" Marco said. "What the hell…"

He didn't stick around to see what Marco had to say.

He couldn't waste any time.

He ran.

He raced down the street, as fast as he could, towards the spot where he'd left Sophie. Rex's weight pressed down on his shoulders, slowing him down.

And as much as he didn't want to let Rex go, as much as he didn't want to be separated from him… he knew he needed his full speed to be able to find Sophie right now.

He untied Rex from his back.

Lowered him down to the ground.

Stroked his fur as he looked up at him with those big, wide eyes.

"I'll come back for you," Billy said. "I promise."

Rex looked up at him, tilted his ears, wagged his tail. Drool dribbled from his jaws.

"Billy?" It was Marco. Running towards him. Gasping for breath. "What's—what's happening?"

"It's Sophie," Billy said, running again. "They took Sophie."

"Who took Sophie?"

"I don't know. But I'm going to find out. Watch him. Okay?"

Marco shook his head. "What—"

"Just fucking watch him."

Marco looked like he was going to argue.

And then he just nodded. Sighed. "I'll watch him."

Billy nodded back.

Looked at the snow beneath him.

There was a little mound of snow at his feet where Sophie started making her snow lady.

And then there were footsteps.

Footsteps. And a trail.

Where someone had been dragged.

He followed that trail with his eyes and saw it led right between the houses.

So that was it.

That was where he needed to go.

He ran through the snow, following that trail.

"Come on, Sophie," he said. "I'm coming for you. I promise."

He reached the back garden.

There was nobody there.

And the footprints and the trail had stopped.

Billy stood there. Heart racing. Shit. She had to be close. She had to be over the fence. In those woods behind the houses.

Or...

Shit.

What if she was in one of the houses?

Right on cue, Billy heard something that made all the hairs on his body stand on end.

A scream.

Sophie.

From inside the house to his right.

He turned around. Slowly.

The side door to the house was ajar.

And there was melted snow right inside.

Footprints.

He pushed the door open.

Lifted his rifle.

Stepped inside.

"I'm coming for you, Sophie. I'm coming for you."

The kitchen was damp and smelled like off milk. The drawers were open, and all the cutlery was gone except for the spoons. Someone must've been in here and ransacked the place a long time ago. In the sink, some dirty old pots covered in mould.

From somewhere above, Billy heard footsteps.

He turned around. Pointed his rifle above.

There was somebody up there.

"Sophie," he said.

He pushed the door open.

Walked down the hallway.

Rushed to the bottom of the staircase.

Swung around and pointed his rifle up there, half expecting Sophie's kidnapper to be standing right there, pointing a gun at him.

But nobody was there.

He swallowed a lump in his throat.

Climbed the stairs.

Slowly.

Keeping his rifle ready at all times.

It was silent upstairs now. Which worried him. All kinds of thoughts circled his mind. Maybe they were gone. Or maybe Sophie was...

No.

He didn't have to think like that.

He had to keep focused.

He had to keep going.

He reached the top of the stairs.

Looked around at the four doors around him.

All closed.

All...

Wait.

On the door right in front of him, he saw water drip from the handle.

A little patch right in front of it.

Someone had been here.

Billy's chest tensed up.

Butterflies raced around his stomach.

He lifted his rifle towards that door and walked towards it.

I'm here, Sophie. I'm right here.

He reached the door.

Grabbed the cool handle.

Held his hand there.

Silence inside.

Those images spiralled his mind again.

The thought of finding her dead in there.

The thought of finding they'd done something awful to her like that blonde girl on the road outside.

And he knew there was only one way to find out.

He swallowed the sickly lump in his throat.

Lowered the handle.

And he pushed the door open.

He saw Sophie right away.

But not just Sophie.

Sophie sat on a pink double bed. The windows of this house were covered.

And the room absolutely reeked.

It didn't take Billy long to realise why.

There were five blonde girls, just like Sophie, sitting in various positions around the room. At first, Billy thought they were mannequins or something like that.

But he soon realised when he smelled the stench of rot and decay that they weren't mannequins at all.

They were dead.

A shiver crept up his spine.

Nausea grew in his chest.

He couldn't stand around here.

He had to get Sophie out of here.

Fast.

"Sophie," he said, walking towards her, rifle still raised. "It's okay. I'm... I'm here."

He rushed towards Sophie, who sat there, wide-eyed, staring at him. Frozen.

And then he heard something behind him.

Movement.

He froze.

There was somebody behind him.

He didn't have time to think.

He swung around with his rifle.

But before he could shoot, he felt a crack, right against the back of his skull, and he fell to the bedroom floor.

CHAPTER THIRTY-FIVE

Billy lay flat on the bedroom floor, and a crippling pain burst through his skull.

His vision was blurry. All he could see was the brown carpet of the floor beneath him. It could be the middle of the night because the windows were all boarded up. But he knew it was day outside. Middle of the afternoon.

The horrible stench in the air hung in his lungs and made him want to throw up.

And it just reminded him of what he'd found in here.

Those girls.

Girls, just like Sophie.

Just like the one on the road.

And now, here he was.

Lying on the floor.

Back of his head aching like mad after being cracked across the skull.

And knowing damn well he needed to get the hell up and get Sophie out of here.

He pushed himself up. He still had his rifle in his hands. He had to get up, and he had to shoot whoever this kidnapper was. He had to—

Another crack across the back of his head.

Ringing in his ears.

A burning pain right across his skull.

The taste of blood in his mouth.

He tried to turn over. Tried to flip onto his back. Even though his vision was blurred, he had to see who was above him.

He had to see them, and he had to stop them.

He went to push himself up and turn around when suddenly, someone grabbed his hair.

They tugged it. Hard.

Pulled his neck right back, so it was exposed.

And then they pressed a knife to his throat.

"Not another move."

He was surprised to hear a woman's voice. Not that it surprised him there were women out there who were crazy. He'd seen enough of them in this world to know it was a possibility.

But that level of brutality.

That degree of brutality towards those girls…

He wasn't sure why, but it just seemed even more of a bitter pill to swallow coming from a woman.

From someone who *was* just a little girl like them, once.

Billy gritted his teeth. Tried to breathe. "I… I don't think you've left me much fucking choice there, do you?"

The woman pushed the blade harder into Billy's neck.

So hard he swore he could feel the skin slicing away.

"You come here, and you try to take her from me. But you'll never take my Eve away from me. Or—or from my Simon. You'll never take her away."

My Eve. Who the hell was Eve? And Simon? Clearly, whoever this woman was, she had it wrong.

But then she was surrounded by the bodies of lots of blonde girls.

Blonde girls Billy could only assume she'd killed.

So he didn't really think logic or reason was going to work where she was concerned.

He cleared his throat. Tried to keep hold of his rifle, even though he knew he couldn't turn around right now. Not with that knife so hard to his neck. "I... I hate to be the bearer of bad news. But this kid. It's not... She's not your Eve."

The woman pushed the knife down harder and let out a cry.

"It's my Eve. It's—it's my Eve! It has to be my Eve!"

She let out another cry. And Billy realised he was dealing with someone very deranged here. Someone very twisted.

And it reminded him of that day with Aoife.

Trapped in that pub with that man whose name he'd forgotten long ago.

The one who'd lost his son.

His son's body across the room, lying there in his bed.

The man convinced Billy was him.

And the sadness around that entire scenario.

He tried to think how Aoife handled that situation. How she navigated her way out of it so calmly.

He felt the danger of the situation building, and he realised this was just a scared woman.

A lost woman.

A terrified woman who'd lost everything.

"I... I know you're hurting," Billy said.

She punched the side of his head. "Shut up."

"I know you're hurting. But... but this girl isn't your Eve."

Another hard punch, right against his right temple. "Shut *up!*"

Billy cleared his throat, the taste of blood welling in his mouth. "She's not your Eve. But that doesn't mean there can't be another... another chance for you. A future for you. And maybe someone else for you."

The woman didn't punch him this time.

She just held on to him.

Gripped his hair tight.

The knife shook against his neck.

"I don't deserve a future," she said.

Billy breathed in deeply through his nose. Tried to stay as calm as possible. "Everyone... everyone deserves a future."

"I don't *want* a future," the woman shouted. "Not without... not without Eve."

Billy swallowed a lump in his throat. "What's—what's your name?"

"I've tried so hard," the woman said, ignoring his question. "So hard to find one like her. And they... they always look like her. They always look just like her. But they're not her. They're never her. And then they upset me and... and it always happens. The accident always happens."

Billy's skin went cold. The realisation—the confirmation—of what this woman had done to these girls sunk in.

She'd murdered them.

She'd abducted them, and she'd murdered them.

All because they looked like her daughter.

All because they weren't her daughter.

"The people with the guns will die for what they've done," she said. "I'll make them pay one day. One day..."

In the horror of the situation, an idea sparked into Billy's mind.

"The people with the guns?" he asked.

"The people in grey. The devils with the guns. The guns... the guns like yours."

"We've lost people because of them, too," Billy said. "We—we can work together. We can fight them. Together. You just have to let us go. Please. You just—you just have to let us go, and we can work through this."

Suddenly, out of nowhere, the woman flipped him over onto his back.

And for the first time, Billy saw her face.

She looked about sixty, but she was definitely younger. Long grey hair. Gaunt face. Bloodshot eyes.

"How can we stop them?" she said. "How—how can you help me?"

Billy lay there, and he felt a sense of sadness. Because for all the horrible things this woman had clearly done... she had got lost along the way. And it was on the Liberators. It was because of their evils that this woman had gone the way she'd gone.

"I don't know how I can help you," Billy said, being as honest as he could be. "But we've both lost because of these people. They've taken so much away from us. So, so much. Let's not let them take our humanity away from us. Not more than they already have."

The woman shook her head.

Tears rolled down her face.

The darkness and the dampness and the smell of the dead all grew, all surrounded Billy and closed in.

"We can—we can stop them," she said.

Billy nodded. "We can."

"We—we can beat them. Together."

"We can," Billy said. "Just... just lower the knife. Lower it. Now. Please."

She nodded.

And then she dropped that knife.

Billy gasped for breath.

The woman tumbled back, crying, wrapping her arms around her knees.

Billy stood up.

He lifted the rifle.

"Billy?" Sophie shouted.

Billy pressed his rifle to the woman's pitiful head.

"Nobody touches Sophie," he said. "Nobody."

The woman looked up at him.

Her eyes widened.

"What—"

And Billy pulled the trigger.

The woman fell back to the floor.

Bleeding from her skull.

Gunshot echoing around the bedroom.

But she was gone.

The woman was gone.

The threat was gone.

Billy lowered his rifle.

He walked over to Sophie.

Lifted her onto his shoulder and walked out of the room towards the darkness.

He looked back.

Back at the bodies of those children.

Back at the woman, a pool of blood stretching around her head.

"Come on," he said. "There's nothing here for us. Not anymore."

And then he closed the door, and he walked away.

Sophie was okay.

And he'd do anything he had to do to keep it that way.

CHAPTER THIRTY-SIX

Billy held Sophie's hand as the group continued their walk towards Fulton, but the poor kid didn't seem to be saying much at all.

It was grey. The snow had stopped. What was left of it on the ground was melting away, merging with the mud in a far less aesthetically pleasing brown slush. The road was quiet. Empty. The usual sights that didn't even deserve mentioning anymore—rusty cars, overgrown grass, street lamps lying across the street. He didn't get that same feeling he was being watched anymore, either. He knew it was just a hunch, but not having that creepy sense he was being followed definitely counted a lot right now.

It could be bullshit, of course. The Liberators could be right on his tail.

But he had to take things moment by moment.

Step by step.

No point getting ahead of himself and worrying about what might be on the horizon.

And at the same point... no point getting ahead of himself and counting his chickens.

He looked down at Sophie.

She glanced away from him. Tried to make it so he didn't know she'd been looking.

He sighed. She'd been like this since the incident with the woman and the blonde girls back at the house. He knew why. He'd killed that woman. Killed her right in front of Sophie.

The kid had already seen enough death the last few months. Seeing him—someone she trusted, someone she thought was different—murder someone like that wasn't exactly ideal.

Could he have let the woman live?

Could he have let her join his people?

Possibly.

Did she deserve it?

After all the things she'd done?

All the people she'd killed?

Absolutely fucking not.

"Are you going to speak to me?" Billy asked. "Or am I gonna have to keep on chatting to slobber mouth Rex here?"

Sophie kept on looking on towards the road ahead, towards Meg and Marco, who led the way.

Billy sighed. "Look, Sophie. I... I'm sorry for what you had to witness back there. I'm sorry for what happened. But that woman. She'd... she'd done some terrible things. Some downright awful things. I couldn't... I couldn't let her live. Not with the things she'd done."

Sophie stayed silent.

"We can do this if that's what you really want. We don't have to talk. Whatever, that's fine with me. But I just... I'm sorry for what you had to witness. But I had to save you—"

"You had to save me? Or you had to save your people?"

Billy frowned. "What's that supposed to mean?"

Sophie looked up at him now, shot daggers at him. "You keep... you keep saying you made a promise. To fight for your people. For... for Steve. But that woman wasn't... she wasn't the people we're fighting. She wasn't a Liberator. She was just... sad."

"She was a murderer," Billy said. "And if I hadn't stepped in, she'd've killed you too."

"Maybe," Sophie said. "But she didn't. And you—you made her a promise. You said you'd let her come with us. Said people got a second chance. That they... that the bad things they'd done, they didn't have to be forever. And then you killed her. Which is... which is just what the Liberators would do. It's just what the bad people would do."

Billy's stomach sank. He felt like shit. He didn't mean to tarnish his image of himself in Sophie's eyes, he really didn't. But he had no regrets about killing that woman. Moral grey area or not, he'd done what had to be done. "I apologise for what you had to witness. But I don't apologise for what I had to do."

"And what will you do when we get to this Fulton place? If it's —if it's even a place at all? What happens when we get there and —and then you know the Liberators are still out there?"

"Sophie, we've been through this..."

"I know... I know you just want to protect me. I know you just want to save me. Because that's what you promised. But... but maybe the best way is by... by just starting again."

Billy gritted his teeth. "I... I can't rest knowing they're out there."

"Then you'll never rest. 'Cause there's always people out there."

Billy felt a knot tightening in his chest. Sophie was right. She might be young, but she had a mature head on her shoulders. Frighteningly so. She was right. He would never rest. Not after what these people had done to Steve. Not after the way they'd destroyed his community. Destroyed his home.

And as hard as it was to give up the fight with the Liberators... maybe it was the only choice he had.

If he really wanted to save his people—and he *was* one of those people—then maybe the best thing would be to start again. With Sophie. In Fulton. Fully put the past behind him.

He swallowed a lump in his throat. Nodded. "I hear you. And I am sorry about that woman. Really. I know... I know sometimes these things are complex. You know that too. But I was just..."

"It's okay," Sophie said. "I know. She... she would've killed me. You saved me. Thank you. I just... I just don't want you to think you—you have to keep on saving everybody."

Billy took a deep breath. Half-smiled. "That's something I'm going to have to get through at my own pace."

Sophie looked back at him. Half-smiled too.

"Hey. You two. Over here."

Billy's stomach sank when he heard Meg's voice.

He turned around.

Saw the pair of them standing there, at the top of this old motorway bridge, looking down towards something.

"Here we go," Billy said.

He walked with Sophie by his side and Rex on his shoulders towards Meg and Marco. He didn't know what the problem was. But he figured there would be a problem. Because there always fucking was, right?

He reached their side. "What is it?"

Marco looked up at him.

Smiled.

"Look," he said.

Billy frowned. "What're you..."

He looked down the length of the motorway, and in the distance, he saw something.

There was a wall.

A tall metal wall, taller than any he'd ever seen.

He couldn't see what was behind it.

But he knew for sure this was unlike any place he'd ever seen.

And he knew for sure it could only be one place.

"Fulton," Billy said.

Meg looked over at him. Smile on her face.

"We're here," she said. "We made it."

CHAPTER THIRTY-SEVEN

Tristan tried to put one foot in front of the other, but he didn't have the strength left in his body to go much further.

He collapsed. Hit the ground, face first. He saw black and tasted cold mud and icy snow. His mouth was dry. It was always dry these days. His legs were absolutely knackered, and he couldn't stop shaking. He could hear footsteps marching beside him. Footsteps he used to march along with. Footsteps that used to give him reassurance. Used to give him a sense of community. A sense of belonging.

Footsteps that now filled him with fear.

He lifted his head. Squinted into the distance.

He saw his fellow—or former—Liberators walking along either side of him, ahead of him, getting further and further down this road. The sight of their grey uniforms filled him with terror. He shivered, completely naked. He had no idea how he was still alive. But then he figured that was something of a skill of these people. They knew how to kill. Boy, did they know how to kill.

But they also knew how to keep you *just* alive, too. When it suited.

Just barely alive. Enough to make sure your very existence was doused in suffering.

That's the life Tristan had been living for... well. He didn't know how long exactly. God knows how damned long it'd been at this point.

But he was living this almost life.

He didn't know how much longer he had left. How much more he had in the tank.

But he knew the day they decided to show mercy on him would be the day they'd achieved everything they could possibly achieve by keeping him alive.

Showing other potential traitors exactly what sort of life they'd be living if they chose the same path.

He felt a hand on his back. "Come on."

Someone dragged him up to his feet.

He tried to hold his ground. His legs were wobbly. His knees were weak. And he couldn't stop shivering. Couldn't stop shaking.

The guard spun him round.

Grabbed him by his throat.

Peered right into his eyes. "I told you to keep fucking moving, traitor."

And then he spat right in his face.

Punched him right in the gut.

Tristan hobbled over. Gasped as the air disappeared from his lungs. A stitch crept up his stomach and into his chest. He couldn't breathe. He tasted blood.

Before he could steady himself, the man dragged him up again so he was standing tall.

Grabbed his throat again.

"Walk," he barked.

He spun Tristan around, and he pushed him like he weighed nothing at all. And Tristan figured he didn't. He'd lost shitloads of weight since being kept prisoner of the people he used to serve. Long,

long days with no food or water. Then suddenly, someone coming to his cell door. Holding hot food. The smell of cooked meat. The promise of succulent, enriching water right at the back of his throat.

And then they spat in it.

Or they pissed in the water.

Or they shat on the food a little.

And the worst thing about it?

Tristan was too exhausted and too starving, and too dehydrated to resist.

So he'd chewed down on that shit-laden food.

He'd drank that piss-infused water.

He'd felt the blobs of spunk clinging to the back of his throat as he tried to swallow the squirrel or rabbit they'd brought for him.

Just enough to keep him alive.

But just enough to make him suffer.

He walked. Walking wasn't easy. Lifting one foot and placing it in front of another was a challenge. He hadn't walked like this in months. His legs were thin. He didn't feel physically capable of keeping his body upright.

But he knew it was in his best interests to keep on going.

To keep on suffering through this torture.

Because if he didn't... the torture would only get worse.

He heard a whimper. Looked around to his right.

And he saw her.

The woman.

The woman with the chain around her neck.

The woman with the sores in the corners of her eyes.

The woman who was constantly crying.

He didn't know who she was. Only that she was guilty about something. Very fucking guilty about something. A prisoner they'd taken. One of the women who would be a part of the new world order.

Someone the General truly believed would fit the bill as a breeder.

Tristan felt sick.

The fact he'd been on board with this for so many years. It made him want to cry.

Not for himself. He was way, way beyond pity for himself.

But for everyone else.

Everyone who'd died.

But more for the people who'd been kept alive.

For the lives they were going to be led towards.

He went to put another foot in front of the other when suddenly, he felt someone holding him back, and he stopped.

He frowned. Stopping him? Why were they stopping him? What did they have in store for him next?

And then he looked around, and he realised everyone had stopped.

None of the Liberators were moving.

All of them were standing there.

Staring ahead.

Tristan squinted into the distance.

And he saw exactly what they were looking at.

There was a motorway ahead of them.

On that motorway, abandoned cars from years ago. Tall weeds cracking through the unkept roads. A few skeletons lying dead on the tarmac.

But it wasn't the motorway that caught Tristan's eye.

In the distance, he saw the walls.

The tall metal walls.

And he knew what this place was.

The place they'd been building up to.

The place they'd been building everything towards.

Fulton.

He looked at those walls in the distance, and he knew it was almost over.

He knew the end was close.

Very close.

And then he saw them in the street.

The little dots in the distance.

People.

Walking towards Fulton.

He couldn't see properly, but he swore he saw one of them.

A man with a girl by his side and a dog on his shoulders.

CHAPTER THIRTY-EIGHT

Billy saw the walls getting closer and closer ahead, and he couldn't shake the feeling something was going to go wrong.

The skies had cleared. It was bright now. Bright blue. The sun beamed down from above, making everything seem so perfect, so happy. The air was cold, and his breath frosted in front of him. The motorway was empty. Silent. Still. So, so still.

And Billy couldn't turn away from those walls in front of him.

And he couldn't shake the butterflies fluttering around in his stomach.

The nervous excitement building.

The walls towered over him. They were just like the ones he'd been told about by Aoife and Kayleigh. The walls that housed communities.

Communities with order.

With structure.

With *power*.

And seeing this community right here, hiding in plain sight... Billy had no idea how he'd managed not to notice it for so many years. But then the country was a whole lot bigger now, wasn't it?

Places that used to take no time at all to get to in a car would take forever on foot.

He figured it made sense. Total sense.

And yet...

The thought that a place like this had been sitting right here for God knows how long?

It was crazy.

But he was here.

He'd made it.

He'd actually made it.

He didn't know what awaited behind these walls. He didn't know if the community here would welcome them or turn them away. He didn't know a thing.

But he was here.

That was the main thing.

That was what counted.

He felt Sophie's hand tighten.

Looked around.

She smiled up at him. Her eyes twinkling in the sunlight.

He smiled back at her. "Almost there."

He looked around again. The tall metal walls of this place just kept on catching his eye. It seemed unreal. Like something out of a sci-fi film. He couldn't wrap his head around how something like this could've been built amid a blackout.

But here it was.

Powered?

Did it really matter?

He'd survived the bulk of his life without power. Power was the dream, sure. It was the heaven he sought. The holy grail *everyone* sought.

But as long as he found a new home—somewhere Sophie could be safe—then did it matter, really?

He felt Rex's weight on his shoulders, as per usual. Heard him panting right by his ear. He smiled. "Never thought you'd see a place like this again, did you? Reminding you of when you were with Aoife, hmm?"

Rex whined a little. Wriggled around on Billy's back, which didn't make things comfier.

But Billy wasn't complaining.

He was just so happy to have made it here.

A knot tightened its grip on his stomach.

A thought raced into his mind.

The Liberators.

Still out there.

Still destroying communities.

Still murdering innocent people.

Still conducting their awful, savage reign of terror.

He took a deep breath. Swallowed a lump in his throat.

One day, Billy. One day. But today is about Sophie. Today is about those closest to you. And today is about you.

That's what Steve would truly have wanted.

"I guess they don't have a doorbell or anything," Marco said.

Billy looked around at him. Smiled. "You can go first if you want to. Give that metal wall a big old knock."

Marco raised an eyebrow. "Me? Uh uh. I've dodged death enough to last nine lifetimes. Maybe you should send Rex over there. He's on his last legs anyway. Well. He isn't even on his legs anymore. You get my point."

Billy shook his head. "Not a chance. Rex's life is way, way more valuable than yours is."

Marco snorted. "Truly charming."

Billy smiled. "So, Meg. I'm guessing this is the place you were telling us about?"

Meg narrowed her eyes. "Are you always this insufferable when you're happy?"

"I don't know about happy. Or insufferable. But... but definitely nervous."

"Yeah," Meg said. "That makes two of us."

"Make that three," Marco said.

"I'm not nervous," Sophie said.

"Well, three against one," Marco said. "Majority rules."

Billy looked at that tall metal wall. He looked down at the gate, right in the middle of the motorway. He didn't see any guards there, watching it. He knew that any moment now, he could see a bullet come racing towards his skull. He knew he could be snuffed out at any second now. He had no idea what he was walking towards.

He was just acting on faith.

On hope.

"Well," Billy said. "No point standing here and waiting around."

"Absolutely fucking not," Marco said.

"Language," Sophie said.

"Oh. My manners. Absolutely shitting not."

Sophie laughed. Marco laughed. Even Meg laughed.

And as Billy stood here with this weird bunch of people who he never for one minute expected he'd end up aligned with, and with his disabled dog dangling from his shoulders, he couldn't help smiling.

"Let's go," he said. "Let's..."

That's when he heard it.

The gunshot.

And then, right beside him, a scream.

CHAPTER THIRTY-NINE

Billy heard the scream.

The blue afternoon skies above were perfect. The perfect winter's day. The stage was set beautifully for the moment.

For reaching Fulton.

For walking up to those walls and finding their new home.

Only...

That bang.

That bang resonating in his skull.

Ringing in his ears.

And the scream that followed.

Hairs crept up his arms. There was a sense of inevitability about that bang and that scream. A sense that... something was bound to happen. That something was always going to happen. Because that's the way it always went, wasn't it?

Billy heard the screaming beside him, and he didn't want to look.

He didn't want to see.

He didn't want to know.

But he had to.

He looked to his left and saw Sophie.

She was holding onto his hand.

Her eyes were wide.

As was her mouth,

She was screaming.

Screaming at the top of her lungs.

But she was alive.

She was still alive.

For now.

He didn't want to look where she was looking. He didn't want to see what she was screaming at.

But he knew he had to.

Because as much as he didn't want to face up to the possibility of losing somebody else... Billy knew time was of the essence right now.

He took a deep breath.

Swallowed a lump in his throat.

Turned around.

Meg was standing. Her eyes were wide. She was staring at something on the road beside her.

It took Billy no time at all to realise what it was.

Or *who* it was.

Marco.

His skull was cracked. Burst open by the bullet. His body was twitching. Foam drooled out of his mouth, and blood and brain slurped out of his skull.

The worst thing about it?

Marco should be dead.

But he wasn't.

He was gargling.

Letting out this deathly gargle that sounded like a cow being slaughtered.

A croaky, desperate gasp for air as he tried to cling to his life.

And seeing him right here like this, bleeding out on the road, he realised something else.

The shot.

It must've come from behind.

He swallowed a lump in his throat.

He turned around.

On the motorway bridge behind him—the one he'd walked along not long ago at all—he saw the figures standing there.

Staring down the length of the motorway towards him.

The figures were dressed in grey.

They were all holding rifles.

He had no doubt at all about who these people were.

"Liberators," Billy said.

Another gasp from Marco. Another grunt. A pained gargle. Agony.

Billy turned around. Holding on to Sophie's hand. Rex on his back. Meg standing there, wide-eyed, clearly terrified.

He looked down at Marco.

Marco's hand was outstretched.

Reaching out towards him.

His fingers twitching.

Like he was reaching out for help.

Billy's stomach sank. Because he knew what he had to do. He knew what the kindest thing to do right now was. He couldn't think about it. He couldn't deliberate over it. He didn't have time to.

"Look away, Sophie," Billy said.

"What?"

"Just look away. Please."

He didn't have time to see whether she looked away or not.

He lifted his rifle.

Held his breath.

Pointed it at Marco, who lay there, writhing, shaking.

"I'm sorry, mate," Billy said. "But—but I know this is what you'd want."

And then he put another bullet into his head.

A bang.

A yelp from Marco, just for a second.

And then he was silent.

Then, he was still.

Billy heard more gunshots from behind.

Bullets blasting into the street around them.

And he knew they didn't have time to hang around here.

"Come on," he said. "We've got to go."

He dragged Sophie in front of him, and he pushed Meg in front, and he ran.

Ran down the road as fast as he could.

Towards that metal wall.

Towards that gate.

He had to get there.

He had to—

An explosion.

An explosion right beside him.

A bullet smashing against the metal door of the car right by his side.

He froze. He knew he couldn't keep running onwards. Because if he kept going, another of his people would be shot. Rex would be shot.

And maybe, just maybe, *he* would be shot.

They'd surely be willing to break their promise to Faye of not killing him if it was from this range, right?

He pulled Sophie to the right, launched himself behind a lorry. "Meg," he shouted. "Come on."

Meg stood there.

Looking back towards the motorway bridge.

"Meg!" Billy shouted. "There's no..."

Another bang.

Meg's head snapped to one side.

Her neck cracked.

Sophie screamed again.

"Meg!" Billy shouted.

He went to launch himself forward towards her, and he stopped himself.

Stopped himself as he stood there, Sophie's hand in his, Rex on his shoulders.

Meg wobbled on her feet.

She collapsed on the road.

Her head cracked against the concrete, making an echo.

He looked down at her body as blood pooled around it, and he felt an emptiness building inside. He felt sadness and a shock deep within.

Because they'd been close.

They'd been so, so close.

And now...

Marco.

Meg.

Gone.

Both of them gone.

He held Sophie tight. Stroked Rex, who whined on his shoulders. And he listened to those gunshots cracking against the cars along the motorway.

"It'll be okay," he whispered. "I... I promise it'll be okay."

He had no idea how long he sat there with Sophie and Rex, watching more blood trickle out of Meg's stationary body.

He had no idea how long he tried to speak to them both, tried to reassure them both.

And he had no idea how long he waited there as the gunshots slowed to a halt, one, by one, by one.

But when the silence fell over the motorway and the shock started to build, Billy didn't have time to even begin processing things.

Because he heard another explosion.

A louder explosion.

He turned around to where the noise came from, and his stomach dropped to new depths.

The metal walls of this Fulton safe haven were on fire.

Smoke rose from the debris.

Little dots of people started to appear, peppering gunshots back towards the Liberators.

And then, emerging from the echo of the explosion, Billy heard a familiar sound.

A sound that reminded him of Eastbrook three months ago.

A sound that haunted his dreams.

Billy heard the screams of a community.

And he knew it was already too late.

CHAPTER FORTY

Billy looked down the slope at the fires in the distance, and he felt a tear roll down his face.

It was night. Pitch black. Freezing cold. So cold he could feel the air, bitter in his lungs.

And he could smell the smoke, too.

Hear the screams.

See the fires rising from Fulton.

And there was absolutely nothing he could do but watch.

He felt frozen to the spot. He couldn't move if he wanted to. He couldn't even feel Sophie's hand in his anymore. Only coldness.

Coldness where she usually held on so tightly.

Coldness where she'd let go.

He could hear her beside him. She wasn't speaking. Or maybe she was. He wasn't sure. He couldn't focus. Couldn't concentrate on anything.

Anything other than that rising smoke.

Anything other than the screaming.

And anything other than the memory of what'd happened today.

Of how events had unfolded.

A shiver crept up his spine.

Approaching the walls of Fulton.

Hopeful.

Optimistic.

Excited.

And then the gunshots.

Sophie's screaming.

Marco falling to the ground.

Billy having to finish him off.

And then running away, and Meg being shot, and…

He closed his eyes. Wiped the tears away.

Opened his eyes again and took a breath of that cold, smoky air.

He could see the fires burning in the distance, and it filled him with terror. The thought of what those people in Fulton were going through. He'd heard a lot of fighting back initially as he, Rex, and Sophie raced away. Sounded like the Fulton lot were really fighting their corner.

But it still wasn't enough.

In the end, nothing was enough against the Liberators.

Their armies were strong.

Their forces were nigh-on infinite.

There was no stopping them.

At all.

He looked down at Rex as he lay there, head flat on the ground, staring off into the distance. And seeing how old he was now, he wondered when it would be his turn, too.

His turn to die.

And then he looked at Sophie, and he felt a knot in his chest.

She stared out at the fires. The flames reflected in her wide eyes. She wasn't speaking. She hadn't said a word.

He wanted to say so much to Sophie. He wanted to apologise to her for not getting her to safety. For letting her down.

And he wanted to apologise to Steve, too, for failing to fulfil his promise.

He'd failed Eastbrook.

He'd failed Sophie.

He'd failed everyone.

He looked at Sophie and Rex.

And then he looked up at the flames rising in the distance.

"Come on," he said. "It's... it's time to go."

Sophie turned around. Frowned. "Go where?"

He didn't answer.

He *couldn't* answer.

Because there was nowhere to go anymore.

There was nowhere safe from these people.

And there never would be.

It was just a long walk to prolong death at this point.

He walked over to Rex.

Knelt down.

Lifted him up.

He looked around at the burning Fulton community.

I'm sorry I couldn't do better.

And then he turned around, and he walked into the woods and the darkness.

He didn't take Sophie's hand.

ne month later...

BILLY STAGGERED through the snow and wondered how long he had left to live in this world—and whether he'd be alive long enough to see another winter.

It was freezing cold. Another icy morning. All around, he could see the snow on the buildings. The roofs of houses covered in white. The street shining with the ice lying on top of it. It was like an ice rink. Really fucking slippery, all the goddamned time. There was a novelty to it originally. Sophie hadn't quite seen snow or ice like this before, probably in her entire life.

But Billy couldn't see the lightness of it.

He couldn't enjoy it.

Because he couldn't shift his thinking from everything that'd happened.

From everything that he'd lost.

He walked down the middle of the street with no real direction in sight. Rex was by his side now. That was one bonus from all this. Rex was walking again. Wasn't such a cripple after all, so that was progress.

But still, there was just this feeling of failure. This feeling of letting Sophie down.

And the memory.

The memory of what'd happened when they'd approached Fulton.

When they'd got so, so close to hope.

Marco.

Meg.

Both of them dying.

And then this supposed Fulton safe haven being attacked.

Destroyed.

Hope snuffed out in a second.

And what was the point anymore? What was the point in anything anymore when there wasn't anything to work towards? When nowhere was safe?

What was the point of even trying when everyone was dying, and when death was going to catch up with him and Sophie and Rex eventually?

Because it would. In time, it would.

The Liberators would catch up with them.

They'd destroy them and their home, wherever it was they settled.

And there was nothing he could do to fight them.

There was nothing he could do to resist.

There was nothing he could do to save his people because his people were gone.

"Is this just how it's going to be now?"

He stopped. Sophie. She hadn't spoken much lately. He could tell she was depressed, too. Tell she was down about all this. And whereas once he might've comforted her and reassured her... he didn't see much use in that anymore, either.

Because what was the point of building up her hopes falsely only for them to come crashing right back down again?

Surely that wouldn't be fair?

He looked around. Saw her standing there, staring at him. She was thin. Always was thin, sure. But right now, she was thinner than he'd ever seen her.

"Sophie," he said. "We've... we've been through this."

But whereas usually she just nodded and accepted that they just had to carry on, moving from place to place, no real direction in sight... today wasn't one of those days.

She shook her head. "I can't... I can't just accept this is all there is."

Billy still couldn't get over how mature she was. Old beyond her young years. Which, in a way, made it even worse for her. The fact she understood what was happening. The fact she saw what was going on. The way her hope was drifting away, slowly but surely. "It doesn't matter whether you accept it or not, kid. It is how it is. If you don't accept it, you're just making shit harder for yourself.

"You've given up," Sophie said.

Billy frowned. "What?"

"You've... you've given up. Completely. On everything."

"It's not about whether I've given up or not. I'm just... What is it you even want?"

Sophie opened her mouth. Closed it. Seemed to spend a few seconds mulling it over, really thinking about whatever she was going to say next.

And then: "I... I feel like you've given up on the thing you promised you'd never give up on."

Billy took a deep breath. His heart racing. "And what's that?"

She looked at him, right in the eyes, and she said the words he dreaded hearing. "Your people."

A knot tightened in Billy's chest. He shook his head. Because he couldn't take that. He couldn't accept it. "I'm here. Fighting. Fighting for you."

"You're not... you're not fighting anymore," Sophie said.

Billy shook his head. "Leave it, Sophie."

"You're just... you're existing. Because you're afraid. Afraid of losing me too. So you'd rather just... you'd rather just pretend there's nothing for us because you're scared of losing everything—"

"I said, leave it!"

He shouted. Didn't mean to, but he shouted. His voice echoed against the empty houses around him. He could hear some birds flapping away nearby.

And Sophie just stood there, staring at him with wide, tearful eyes.

But he couldn't help himself.

"You know what? You're right. Maybe it would've been better if we'd all died back at Eastbrook. Because that's all that's gonna happen anyway. That's all that's coming for all of us. And there's nothing I can do to change that."

Sophie shook her head. "That's—that's not true."

"Then maybe you should just go fucking make it on your own, seeing as you know so fucking much about surviving."

He regretted those words the moment he said them.

He didn't mean what he'd said. He was just trapped. And confused. And lost.

But it was too late for him to take those words back.

He could see that from the look in Sophie's eyes.

"Sophie..." he said.

But she didn't give him a chance to say anything else.

She turned around.

Walked away.

He stood there, staring at the side of the house she'd disappeared down. He looked down at Rex, who stared up at him, judgement in his eyes. "What?" he said. "Don't give me that look."

But as he stood there, staring at Rex, it became clear.

Everything became clear.

Everything Sophie said was right.

Because this was about not wanting to lose what he already had.

But by living the way he was living, by drifting from place to place, he was giving up on the very ones he'd promised to fight for.

Sophie.

Rex.

But also... himself.

He looked around to the side of that building where Sophie had disappeared, and he felt a sudden surge of energy.

A sudden life springing into his body.

"Sophie," he said. "I..."

And then he stopped.

He stopped because up ahead, he saw them.

Liberators.

Marching towards him.

They were here.

CHAPTER FORTY-TWO

Billy stood in the middle of the road and stared up at the Liberators in the distance, marching down the hill towards him.

There weren't as many of them as he'd seen before. But it was definitely them. The grey he recognised. The way they marched, in such order, such cohesion. It sent shivers up his spine. He hadn't seen these fuckers for so long, and now here they were, heading right towards him.

He saw them, and he felt anger in the pit of his stomach.

Anger deep in his gut.

He tightened his grip on the rifle he'd stolen from that Liberator back at Eastbrook all those months ago now.

And as he stood there, he saw all options lining up before him.

Finding a vantage point in one of these houses around him.

And then shooting at them.

Standing in a window and wiping out as many of the bastards as he possibly could.

A chance for revenge.

A chance to get revenge for the death these people had caused.

Because it didn't matter if it was only a few of them. It didn't matter if it made no real difference in the grand scheme of things.

It mattered to *him*.

After the death and murder and destruction they'd caused.

After the horrible ways they'd sent his life spiralling and changed everything in ways he dreaded to even think about... he deserved some degree of revenge.

Rex growled beside him. The cold winter air blew against his face, making him shiver. His heart beat faster. He tightened his grip on his rifle. He had to be ready to fire. He had to be ready to *fight*.

And then something else came to mind.

Sophie.

She'd gone. Walked away. After he made that shitty comment to her. Snapping in the moment.

He thought about what she'd told him. About how he was just afraid to lose someone else.

He knew how right she was. He saw it now. Clearly.

She was his people.

It might not have been the mass of people Billy *wanted* to save at Eastbrook and beyond. But protecting her was his absolute priority now. It had to be.

So he had to get to her.

He had to find her.

And then he could go from there.

"Sophie!" he called.

He ran down the street, staring at the Liberators at all times. Watching them walk further and further down the road. Still hard to tell how many of them there were exactly. But too many. Far too many breathing the same air as him.

He'd put a stop to that.

But no...

Sophie first.

He ran down the side of the house he'd seen Sophie walk down, and he froze.

There was no sign of her.

"Sophie?" he said.

He walked down through the snow. He could see her footsteps. But as he listened to those footsteps resounding in the distance, getting closer, he couldn't shake the feeling he had inside right now.

The feeling that something was wrong.

An eerie feeling sending shivers up his spine.

Where was she?

"Sophie?" he said, walking down the gap between the houses. The hair on the back of his neck stood on end. Not now. Not fucking now...

But the further he got down that path, the more his sense of dread grew.

The more he felt like something was wrong.

Very, very wrong.

"Where's she at, Rex?" he muttered. "Where's she..."

And then he stopped.

Because he saw them.

Right in front of him.

Just like he'd seen before when Sophie went missing four months ago.

Footprints.

Two sets of footprints.

But something else, too.

Blood.

He looked down at those specks of blood, and his body went cold.

His stomach turned inside out.

They had her.

They had her, and they'd taken her.

He stood there, and as his heart beat faster and faster, as the footsteps marched closer and closer, he felt dread crowd his system.

Sophie was gone.

Someone had taken her.

And the Liberators were closing in.

CHAPTER FORTY-THREE

Sophie saw someone standing before her the second she stepped into the alleyway.

It was a girl. She looked no older than her. Wide eyes. Staring at her with tears running down her cheeks. She wasn't wearing much. She looked frozen to the bone.

And as Sophie stood there, a shiver ran up her spine.

Because this girl looked like her.

Blonde, just like her.

She stood there and stared at this girl as the cold wind sent goosebumps down her arms.

She knew she should call for Billy.

She knew she should tell him to come here and check this out.

But this girl...

This poor girl.

"Hel—hello?" she said.

The girl didn't say anything back to her.

She just stared at her with those wide, bloodshot eyes.

Watching.

Snow sprinkled down from above. A cold breeze gusted

through the alleyway. Sophie felt frozen. Rooted to the spot. The houses towered over her on either side. In one of the windows, up to her left, she swore she saw movement.

She stood there, and she heard something. Footsteps. Marching her way. And then a voice. "Sophie!" Shouting. Billy.

She heard him shouting, and then she heard something else, too.

More footsteps.

A long way away. Well in the distance.

But heading this way.

Footsteps, and lots of them.

She turned around. Squinted over to where she swore she could hear those footsteps.

She couldn't see where they were coming from. Not between these houses.

But a knot tightened in her stomach.

She'd heard footsteps like that before.

She'd heard marching like that before.

The Liberators.

She glanced back at the girl, and something made her skin crawl.

She was gone.

Sophie stood there. Very still. Heart racing. Chest tight.

She couldn't see the girl anymore.

Only her footprints.

Leading around the back of the house.

She heard Billy and Rex getting closer, and she knew she should wait for them. She knew she should tell him about what she'd seen.

Because this didn't feel right.

Something didn't feel right about this at all.

But she took a deep breath.

And she walked.

Walked around the back of the house.

Following those footprints.

Closely.

She could taste vomit in the back of her throat. She couldn't stop shaking.

That girl.

Whoever she was...

She needed to find her.

She couldn't just let her go.

"Sophie!"

Billy again. She knew she should call back to him.

But she was too focused on what was ahead of her.

Too focused on these footprints.

Too focused on this girl.

She reached the edge of the footprints.

Reached the back of the house.

And a part of her didn't want to look around the corner.

A part of her didn't want to see.

But she had to.

She couldn't just stand here.

She couldn't just walk away.

She had to look.

She took a deep breath.

And then she stepped around the corner.

Towards the back of the house.

She looked down the yard area at the back of this house, and a shiver ran up her spine.

The girl stood there.

But this time, she wasn't crying.

She was smiling.

She lifted a hand and placed a finger in front of her lips. "Ssh."

Goosebumps spread up Sophie's arms. "What..."

And then she heard it.

Shuffling right behind her.

A crack, right across her head.

A bolt of pain.

And then everything went muffled and dark, and she fell to the snowy floor, and...

CHAPTER FORTY-FOUR

Billy stared at the footprints and the blood on the snow, and he heard the Liberators closing in.

The sky was grey. The air was cold. All Billy could stare at was this patch of blood in front of him, right between these two houses.

Sophie was gone.

Out of nowhere, just like that, Sophie was gone.

And in her place?

Footprints and blood.

His heart raced. The sound of the Liberators' footsteps getting closer sent a shiver up his spine. He knew he couldn't afford to stand around here and wait. They'd be here in no time. And when they found him... fuck knows what would happen.

And at the same time, he wanted to shoot them down. He wanted to kill every last one of those fuckers. It'd be the smallest thing he could do to level the stakes after what they'd done to his people, after what they'd done to him, after the life they'd forced him to live for all these months.

For the life they'd forced Sophie to live.

A life no child deserved.

But he knew, standing here, that he couldn't even think about the Liberators right now.

He could only think about Sophie.

"Sophie," he muttered.

He walked along this path of footprints. Followed them around the back of the house on the left, Rex close by his side. His heart raced even harder with every step he took. He saw more specks of blood. She was in danger. Big, big danger.

He didn't know who had her. But something told him it wasn't the Liberators.

If he didn't hurry the hell up, they'd be here soon too.

And then they were in deep, deep fucking shit.

"Sophie!" he called.

But again, his voice just echoed off into the distance.

Swallowed up by the silence.

Snow falling heavier.

The sound of his own heavy breathing filling his mind.

"Come on," he said. "Don't do this. Not right now. Don't fucking..."

He stopped.

The back door to this house on his left.

It was ajar.

And he saw something that made him shiver.

Footprints.

And the blood.

He looked up at that door.

Pointed his rifle at it.

They were in there.

Sophie was in here.

But he had to be careful.

He had to be quiet.

He couldn't take any chances.

Couldn't take any risks.

He looked over to his left. He knew his window of escape from the Liberators was going to disappear very, very soon.

And his opportunity to take them out was going to disappear, too.

But that didn't matter.

What mattered was finding Sophie.

Saving Sophie.

Getting her the hell out of whatever mess she'd found herself in.

He took a deep breath.

"Come on, Rex," he said. "She can't be far away."

And then he stepped in through the back door.

He clutched his rifle. Looked around this messy kitchen. It was a real shithole. Smashed plates everywhere. Rotten old food that looked like it'd gone off a long time ago. Absolutely reeked of shit in here, too. Shit and off milk, and maybe a hint of a dead body.

Which filled Billy with fear.

He walked across the creaky kitchen floor.

Over to the door to the hallway.

More footprints, leading right around to the lounge.

More blood.

He swallowed a lump in his throat and walked down that hallway.

Rifle raised.

He had to be ready for whatever he came across.

He had to be ready for anything.

He walked over to the lounge door.

Stopped right in front of it.

Took a deep breath.

"Here goes nothing," he said.

And then he pushed the door open, and he stepped inside.

The lounge was dark. The curtains were drawn, and only a little light peeked through. It was dusty in here. So, so dusty.

And the smell…

Oh God, the smell…

He covered his face instinctively, then put his finger back on the rifle's trigger. Because whoever was in here, they were fucked up, that much was clear. Whoever was in here, he didn't want to risk it around them. He didn't want to mess with them.

But as he looked around, he didn't see anyone at all.

Anything at all.

"Sophie?" he said.

He walked a few steps. He could see where that blood was leading now. Right over to the leather sofa. More of it on the carpet, right in front of it.

He crept towards it, Rex following him closely. Whining a little. Like he was uncomfortable about all this too. Seriously creeped out.

And when he reached that sofa, he stopped.

There was something there.

Something staring up at him.

Something that sent a cold shiver down his spine.

A finger.

A severed finger.

Blood trickling from the back of it.

And right beside it?

A long clump of blonde hair.

Splattered with blood.

He looked down at that finger and those blonde hairs and felt his whole world collapsing into itself when suddenly he heard something that sent a shiver up his spine.

Footsteps.

A cry.

And then the next thing he knew, he felt a heavy crack over his head, and he collapsed to the floor.

CHAPTER FORTY-FIVE

Billy felt the heavy crack against his head and fell to the floor.

He slammed against the floor with a thud. Bit his tongue on the way down and tasted blood right away. His ears were ringing. His vision was blurred. Everything sounded so muffled and so distant. He could hear Rex barking, and he was torn—torn because, on the one hand, he wanted to protect him, and on the other hand, he wanted to stop him barking.

He didn't want the Liberators to hear.

He turned around. Rolled onto his back. Stared up at the person standing above him in the darkness of this lounge.

He couldn't see him properly in the darkness, but he could see he had a long beard. Blond hair, the sort you didn't usually see on blokes. His face was covered in cuts and scratches, and he looked gaunt and emaciated like he hadn't eaten for years.

The man was holding onto a hammer. The hammer had a speck of blood on it.

Sophie was nowhere to be seen.

The man stood over Billy, dripping sweat. He was saying

things, but Billy was so dazed that he couldn't hear him properly at all.

He just held on to that rifle, and he knew he could fire at him.

He could fire at him and gun him down, and it'd be over in a flash.

Completely over...

But...

The Liberators.

Outside.

He couldn't draw attention to himself.

Especially when he didn't know where Sophie was.

Or... well.

Didn't know where Sophie was other than in here somewhere.

He thought about the finger lying on the sofa.

And those strands of long, blonde hair.

He lifted his rifle and went to throw caution to the mother-fucking wind and fire anyway when the man grabbed it and pressed it to his throat.

He crouched down over Billy. Sat on him with all his weight. Pressed the cold metal of the rifle to Billy's neck, making breathing impossible.

"You murdered her," the man spat. "You killed my wife. You killed her in cold blood. In cold fucking blood!"

What the fuck? Who was he talking about? Who had he killed?

"You—you came in our home, and you killed her. And now you'll pay. Now you'll fucking pay."

Billy pushed the rifle back, trying to ease the suffocating pressure on his throat.

Rex barking like mad as the Liberators inched closer and closer.

Come on. You've got this, Billy. You can get out of this. You have to get out of this. You...

And then he saw the girl.

The girl standing there.

In the corner of the room.

Blonde hair.

Blue eyes.

Missing a finger.

But not Sophie.

Not Sophie.

But if it wasn't Sophie, and she looked so alike, then who...

Suddenly, it clicked.

The woman he'd murdered.

The one who'd abducted and killed those blonde kids.

"You murdered my wife," the man spat. "You murdered my Maria."

Billy looked up at this utter nutcase, and he couldn't actually believe it. All this time and it was this guy who'd come back to haunt him?

He remembered the woman a month ago. The one who'd kidnapped Sophie. The one he'd found surrounded by dead girls. Dead *blonde* girls. Going on about her missing daughter, Eve, and how she wanted her back.

He remembered something else she'd said. Something he hadn't thought much of at the time. But something he remembered clearly now.

"Simon," Billy muttered. She'd mentioned a Simon.

And if Billy had a quid to bet with, he'd bet that this was fucking Simon right now.

Fuck. He really could do without this shit right now.

He looked up at the man, right into his eyes, as he pressed down on his neck.

As his breathing got harder and harder.

As his vision grew more blurry.

He glanced over at this kid again. This blonde kid who wasn't Sophie.

The smile on her face.

Like this was some kind of joke to her.

Like she was already too far gone.

He looked around at Simon as Rex barked at him, and for a moment, he had no idea how the hell he was going to get out of this one.

And then he saw it.

To his right.

The coffee table.

The bottle sitting on top of it.

Wine bottle. Empty by the looks of things.

It was all he had.

He reached out. Strained to grab it with his fingertips.

Simon pressed down harder and tighter on his neck.

Smiling, saliva drooling from his lips.

"You thought you were safe, didn't you, huh? You thought you and your little blonde thing would just get away. But you ain't no idea who you've picked a fight with."

Billy stretched further for that bottle.

He was so close his fingertips were just touching the glass.

But Simon pressed so hard he was pretty sure he was crushing his windpipe.

Simon laughed. "We'll look after your little'un. Don't you worry. We'll look after her good. Real good."

He pushed down harder.

Billy felt the glass against his fingertips.

He strained to reach it and...

It slipped from his grip.

Smashed against the floor.

Simon looked around.

Billy looked around.

Felt cool wine touching the tips of his fingers.

Smelled sour grapes.

Simon looked back around at him, and he smiled.

"Nice try," he said. "But you ain't..."

Footsteps.

Footsteps right outside.

Voices.

Simon lifted his head.

And Billy sensed a window of opportunity, and he knew he had no time to think anymore.

He grabbed a piece of the broken glass.

Swung it up, gashing Simon's neck.

Blood spurted out all down his front.

His eyes widened, and he let go of the rifle and clutched his neck, crying as streams of blood spurted out, covering his dirty white shirt.

Billy pushed him back.

He grabbed him.

Didn't give a fuck about Rex's barking anymore.

Didn't give a fuck about the Liberators or anything.

He just needed to know where Sophie was.

"Where is she?"

Simon opened his mouth, blood pooling out, thick and red, almost black.

Billy grabbed his throat and tightened his grip around it.

Felt the hot blood spurting out over his fingers as he squeezed.

Hard.

"I asked you a fucking question. Where is she?"

Simon gasped.

He moved his lips, but no sounds came out.

Billy tightened his grip as hard as he could.

"I won't ask again. If you've any fucking decency about you... if you care about these girls at all... tell me where she is. Right fucking now."

His eyelids fluttered shut.

For a moment, Billy thought it was over. Thought he was dead. Thought time was up.

And then Simon lifted a shaking hand and pointed towards the door.

"Good," Billy said.

He dropped Simon to the floor.

Pushed him back.

And then he lifted a boot.

Hovered it over his neck.

"This is for those children," he said.

And then he stamped down on Simon's neck.

Hard.

A horrible squelching sound filled the air.

He felt the blood sticking against his boots.

He looked down at Simon as he writhed around, silently screaming on the floor.

"I have no regrets about what I did to your wife, you sick fuck," Billy said. "And I'd do it again in a heartbeat."

He booted Simon across the face.

He grabbed his rifle.

And then he rushed over to the lounge door.

He thought about that kid he'd seen. The blonde girl. The one who wasn't Sophie. He felt bad for her. And he hoped wherever she was, she'd be okay. He never believed anyone was ever too far gone. Not with the shit he'd been through and come back from.

But right now... he had an even more urgent goal.

He needed to get to Sophie.

He needed to...

He reached the lounge door when he heard something that filled him with dread.

Footsteps.

A door creaking.

And then more footsteps.

Inside.

He stood there and listened to those footsteps, dread filling his body.

Because he knew what it meant.
He knew exactly what it meant.
They were here.
The Liberators were here.
And they were in the house.

CHAPTER FORTY-SIX

Billy heard the front door creak open,and he heard the Liberators' footsteps creeping into the house, and he couldn't do anything but stand there and hold his breath.

He stood in the darkness of this curtained lounge. The body of the man who'd abducted Sophie and tried to kill him lay twitching on the floor, bleeding out. Billy listened to those footsteps getting closer, creaking their way through the hallway and into the house. Even though he hadn't seen the source of them yet... he knew. He just knew who they belonged to.

Liberators. Absolutely no doubt about it in his mind.

He could tell from the way they were walking.

The way they were getting closer.

Stalking him like he was prey.

Rex stood panting at his side. Little git probably drew them here with his bloody barking. Couldn't really blame him. Only doing his job.

He stood there at the door. The smell of damp filling his lungs. The metallic tang of blood clinging to his lips. His heart racing and his head spinning. He felt dizzy and weak.

He needed to get the hell out of this room and find Sophie.

She was in this house somewhere. He didn't know where exactly, but he knew she was close.

And at the same time, hearing the Liberators' footsteps... he wanted to punish them. He wanted to put them through hell for the things they'd done. For what they'd taken from him. For the pain and the destruction they'd caused.

But then he took another deep breath of that nasty-smelling air.

There would be a time for revenge.

And that time was not right now.

Right now was for rescuing Sophie—and getting the hell out of this place.

He listened to those footsteps, and he stayed still. Very still. He held on to his rifle. He had to be ready to fire. He didn't want to get in a gunfight if he could help it. Needed to keep a low profile. Needed to lay low.

But at the same time... he had to be ready.

He had to be prepared.

His and Sophie's lives might well depend on it.

If she was even alive at all...

No.

Don't think like that.

Don't fucking think like that.

He heard the footsteps right in front of this lounge door.

And right after he heard them, he heard something else that made his stomach sink.

Rex.

Growling.

He looked over at him. Glared at him. Hoping damn well the dog would get the message from that look alone.

But then Rex growled even louder.

Tucked his ears back.

Let out a little whine.

Shit.

Oh shit.

He was going to bark.

He was going to fucking bark.

Billy held his breath and braced himself for the loud noise of Rex's bark to draw the Liberators' attention this way.

And then something remarkable happened.

Rex got down.

He lay flat on his paws and let out a sigh.

Wow. That was... something. Unprecedented. And he'd make damn sure he gave Rex the fuss he deserved for being such a bloody good boy later.

But for now...

He looked back at the door in front of him.

Heard the footsteps walking into the room opposite, whatever it was.

He held his breath, and he knew he needed to act fast.

Before they got in here.

He took a deep breath, and then he opened the door.

He saw the shadow of the Liberator in the room opposite.

He saw the front door. Open. Nobody there. Not right now.

And then he saw the staircase, and he knew he only had one option.

He had to get up there.

He had to find Sophie.

He had to...

Suddenly, right in front of him, he heard a muffled cry.

He wasn't sure where it was coming from. Not at first.

And then it clicked.

The cupboard under the stairs.

Someone was in there.

"Sophie," Billy said.

He went to throw himself at that door when he saw the Liberator's shadow shift in the room opposite.

He saw the Liberator running around towards that cry.

They'd heard her.

They were onto her.

Billy felt himself at a fork in the road.

He needed to get to Sophie.

But if that Liberator stepped out here and found him, he'd be dead.

They'd all be dead.

But what else could he do?

What other option did he have?

What...

And then instinct kicked in.

Another idea sparked in his mind.

He stepped back into the shadows of the dark, curtained lounge.

And he waited.

He saw the Liberator step out of the room opposite.

Walk over towards that cupboard under the stairs.

He saw him lift his rifle.

And he knew he had to act fast.

He knew he had to time this just right.

He had to stay quiet.

He held his breath.

The Liberator stepped around the front of the door to the cupboard under the stairs.

Nerves crippled Billy's stomach.

Just another second. Just another...

And then the Liberator grabbed the handle and opened the door.

Lifted his rifle and pointed it right inside.

And that's when Billy knew he had to act fast.

Billy stepped out of the stuffy, damp room.

He walked up behind the Liberator.

Pressed the rifle to the back of his head.

And as much as he wanted to be stealthy, as much as he

wanted to keep a low profile, Billy only had one choice.

"Not so fast," Billy said.

The Liberator started to turn.

But not fast enough.

Billy pulled the trigger.

A loud bang filled the hallway.

The Liberator's head exploded right before him.

He staggered forward, tumbled into a puddle of his own blood and skull fragments.

And in front of him, staring out at Billy with a big nasty bruise on her forehead and blood trickling through her hair, Sophie.

"Sophie," Billy said.

He threw himself into that cupboard. Yanked the duct tape from her mouth and then from her wrists. "You okay?"

Sophie nodded. "I—I'm sorry. He just—"

"It's okay," Billy said. "It doesn't matter now."

"But I—I shouldn't have—"

"Sophie, it's okay. We just... we just need to get out of here right now. It's not good here. The Liberators are crawling this street. And they're pretty soon gonna realise one of their pals is missing. Come on. We've got to... we've got to go upstairs. Wait this out. It's not safe out there just yet."

He took Sophie's hand, and he ran up the stairs towards the front bedroom.

He crept over to the window.

Crouched and crawled through this dusty old bedroom, which smelled of shit.

He heard the footsteps outside and knew exactly what group this was and who these people were.

"I'm gonna take a look," Billy said. "And when it's safe to make a break... I'll let you know, okay?"

Sophie looked right into his eyes and nodded. "I trust you."

"Good," Billy said.

He turned around.

Held his breath as he crouched under that window.

"Here goes nothing."

And then he popped his head up.

He saw them in the street.

Saw the grey uniforms.

Saw the rifles.

So many of them. More than he'd first thought.

Liberators.

And as he stood there, rifle in hand, he felt a force tugging at him.

A force inside urging him to point his rifle out the window.

Urging him to fire.

He stood there looking down as they passed through the street, and he took a deep breath.

"Not now," he muttered. "Not…"

That's when he saw someone.

Someone who made his stomach turn.

Someone who made his skin turn cold.

No. Wait.

Not just one person. But two people.

One of them was a man. He looked like he'd been beaten to a pulp. He was being dragged along with a chain around his neck. He didn't look like he had much life left in his skinny frame.

It was Tristan.

The Liberator who'd helped him escape Eastbrook four months ago.

But it wasn't just Tristan who caught his eye.

There was a woman there, too.

A woman about his age.

Tall. Slender. Blonde hair. Looked pale and exhausted.

Haunted.

He looked at this woman, and he felt a wave of anger, hatred, but also sadness and pity, too.

Because she had a chain on her neck.

She was right at the front of the group, and she had a chain on her neck, just like other women and children in the middle of this crowd.

He looked down at her, and even though she'd changed almost beyond recognition, he knew exactly who it was.

"Faye," he said.

"What?" Sophie said.

Billy watched the Liberators pass through the street, and he felt torn.

It felt so wrong letting them just walk through like this, transporting slaves by the looks of things.

It felt so wrong just letting Tristan be treated like this, presumably for being a traitor.

And Faye...

As much as he despised what she'd done... he couldn't hate her.

He couldn't just let her go.

He couldn't just let them do this.

"I need..." Billy started. "I need to do something."

"What?"

He stood up. Lifted his rifle without really thinking. Pointed outside. "I need to..."

And that's when he stopped.

That's when he froze.

Because the man standing beside Faye.

The one holding the chain around her neck.

The one wearing black, completely unlike the other Liberators.

He looked around at Billy, right into his eyes, and he smiled.

Billy felt the hairs on the back of his neck stand on end.

Because one by one, more of these Liberators started turning around.

More of them looked up at him.

More of them stared right up at him and Sophie.

He grabbed Sophie's hand. "We need to…"

That's when he heard the floorboards behind him creak.

His stomach sank.

He turned around.

Slowly.

Two men in grey stood there at the door.

Rifles in hand.

Smiles on their faces.

"Hello, Billy," the one on the left said. "I think it's about time you met The General."

CHAPTER FORTY-SEVEN

Billy stood at the window with his rifle in hand and he knew he was in deep, deep shit.

The two Liberators stood opposite him. Holding their rifles. Pointing them at him, Sophie, Rex. And if it wasn't for Sophie and Rex, he might've just risked it. He might've just tried shooting them. Or tried jumping the hell out of the window.

He might've tried getting the revenge he so desperately craved.

But it was like he said.

He had Sophie and Rex to think about.

He couldn't risk anything while they were close.

He stood there and looked at these two men standing in the bedroom with him. They were smiling. Looked totally calm. Which was creepy. There was something glazed about their eyes. Something less than human about them.

And when Billy looked back over his shoulder, out the window, he saw the Liberators in the street all staring up at him, too.

Tristan staring up at him.

Faye staring up at him.

And the man with the chain around Faye's neck.

The man Billy could only assume was the one they called the General.

"It's a simple choice," the man on the left in the room with him said. "You come with us, and we'll figure something out. Or you don't, and... Well. Let's just say it doesn't end well for you. For either of you."

Billy looked around at the pair of them, and he shook his head. "What do you want?"

The man on the left smiled. The other followed. "You're a lucky man to still be alive, Billy. You're alive because we keep our promises."

"To Faye? Is that what this is about?"

The man laughed. "Faye? You really think it's because of Faye that you're still alive?"

Billy felt a shiver creep up his spine.

He had a feeling he knew what this was about.

He had a feeling there was something secret waiting to be unearthed.

Something he didn't want to face up to.

Something he didn't want to accept.

But something he couldn't run from.

"Come with us," the man said. "Come with us, and you get a chance. A chance you've earned. Whether you realise it or not."

Billy looked at Sophie.

Looked at Rex.

Looked at the pair of them, and he shook his head.

"You don't touch the pair of them," Billy said.

The men narrowed their eyes. Didn't say a word.

"The girl. And my dog. You don't touch them. Understand? You don't lay a finger on either of them."

The two men looked at each other.

Then they looked back at Billy, and they nodded.

"I can't speak for the General," the man on the left said. "But if you come in with an open mind... I don't think you need to worry one bit."

Billy shook his head. Kept his rifle raised. He looked at Sophie, and he wanted to apologise to her. He didn't want to put her in any danger. He didn't want to take any chances.

Unless...

Unless he had time to fire at these two men.

To shoot them, right now.

Because what did it matter what this General had to say to him?

What did any of that shit matter?

Faye had betrayed him and his people.

And Tristan... Tristan had made his sacrifice. Tristan had made his choice. And it was a choice that Billy would respect 'til the day he died.

But what else was he hoping to gain?

He stood there, and he felt torn in two directions.

Understanding these people.

Understanding what they wanted.

Trying to bargain with them, somehow.

Or destroy them.

Or the other direction.

The direction that, deep down, he knew was right.

The direction he had promised Steve all those months ago, now.

Protect our people.

Fight for our people.

"Come with us, and we can keep you safe," the man on the left said. "We can protect you all. And we can provide you the shelter and the security you need. You just... need to hear us out. That's the price you have to pay."

Billy stood tall. Rex growled beside him. He saw these two options right in front of him. And as much as he felt torn inside...

deep down, he knew there was only one choice he could make, realistically.

"I made a promise to someone," Billy said. "Someone very close to me."

The man on the left narrowed his eyes.

"I made a promise that I'd do whatever I could to protect my people."

The man stared at Billy closely. "And?"

Billy took a deep breath. "And I've decided that's exactly what I'm going to do."

He didn't even think.

He fired.

Fired a spray of bullets at both of them men.

Bullets slammed into their chests, into their stomachs.

And before they could even register what was happening, he grabbed Sophie's hand. "Come on!"

He ran.

Ran past the two men.

Ran as bullets slammed into the bedroom windows.

Ran as orders were barked.

As Liberators swarmed towards the house.

He ran down the stairs towards the open front door, Sophie's hand in his.

"We've got to..."

And then another Liberator appeared.

He lifted his rifle.

Fired at the man, shooting him right in the head. "Through the back," he said.

He ran with Sophie and Rex.

The Liberators were getting closer.

More of them were in the house.

They were running out of time.

It was getting too late.

But as he ran with Sophie and Rex, he felt a strange sense of certainty about what he was doing.

A strange sense of pride.

He was doing the right thing.

He was making the right choice.

He ran to the kitchen door.

Opened it.

He looked down the empty alleyway. Looked right and saw shadows emerging.

Looked left and saw an opening.

"Quick!" Billy shouted.

He ran down that grass, and Sophie ran, and Rex ran, and he knew they had to keep running now.

He knew this was their life now.

He kept on running when suddenly he turned a corner and saw someone standing right in front of him.

He stopped.

The man in black stood right before him.

There were two Liberators either side of him.

And he was holding something.

A gun.

A gun to Faye's head.

A smile on his face.

"Hello, there," the man said as more of those Liberators ran through the house behind Billy and Sophie, surrounding them. "Allow me to introduce myself. I am the General. And it's a pleasure to finally meet."

CHAPTER FORTY-EIGHT

Billy saw the man called the General, who he'd heard so much about, standing there with the pistol to Faye's head, and he felt time standing still.

He held Sophie's hand. Tightly. All around, he saw Liberators. All with their rifles pointed towards him. He could hear them behind him, approaching from the house he'd just run through. He could hear them everywhere. And as much as he hated to admit it, as much as he hated to face up to it... he knew he was surrounded.

He knew there was no way out.

He stood there, and he stared into the General's eyes. And then at Faye. Tears rolled down Faye's cheeks when she saw Billy. He could see bruises on her neck and under her eyes. And he wanted to scream at her. You happy now? Is this the fucking life you wanted?

But right now wasn't the time for that level of anger.

Right now was the time for getting the hell out of this.

With Sophie.

With Rex.

Nothing else mattered.

"I've heard a lot about you," the General said. He was a tall man. Very bulky. Larger- than-life figure. He absolutely oozed confidence and charisma. Billy could see how such a guy had ended up leading people like this. Even if he was just serving somebody else.

"I've heard a lot about you too," Billy said.

The General smiled. "I am sorry for what we did to your community. Your home. Your people. I hope you understand it's not personal."

"You slaughtered people," Billy said. "Children. You—you slaughtered children."

"We purged the landscape of insurgents," the General said. "And we will keep on doing that. Until we are united. A truly United Kingdom, once again."

"You're insane," Billy said.

"I'm following orders. But truly, I disagree with your conclusions. I am not insane. None of us are insane. We're all just fighting for a better future. For a more united future. A future without conflict. A future without war."

"And that's how you propose we get there? By murdering everyone in your way?"

"If that's what it takes, then yes. That's exactly how we get there."

Billy looked into this man's eyes, and he shook his head. He saw the dead-eyed soldiers behind him. And he realised that no matter how advanced these people were, no matter where they'd come from, or who they served... ultimately, that didn't matter.

What mattered was the girl right beside him.

What mattered was survival.

He wasn't going to win any argument with this man. Or with any of these people.

He looked around at them all, and he wanted to fight to sway them.

But these were murderers.

These were savages.

These people truly believed in their cause.

He lowered his head. And he looked at the ground.

"Don't look so defeated," the General said. "Because we're reasonable people."

"Reasonable fucking people?"

"You can say what you want to say about us. When you look at what humanity has been doing to each other over the years—before you were born, since you were born, and even since the blackout—you can't say unity isn't a noble goal."

"I can say genocide is a fucking twisted goal."

"You can say what you want. Genocide has got humanity to new levels in the past. Do you think we'd even be here today if not for the genocide of your ancestors?"

Billy shook his head. "We're supposed to learn from the past. Not repeat it."

"And that's exactly what we're doing. We've seen where we went wrong. And we're going to make sure we raise a race that will never go wrong again. What goals are purer than that?"

Billy looked into this man's cold blue eyes, and he didn't know what to say. He was honestly speechless. He was a Nazi. A full-blown Nazi.

And it didn't seem to matter what he said. He was cornered.

He was surrounded.

He was in great danger.

He looked at Sophie. Squeezed her hand a little.

Then he looked back at the General. "Tell me what you want. Tell me why I'm still alive."

The General smiled. Still holding his pistol to Faye's head. He smirked like he'd been waiting for Billy to ask him that question for a long time. "We've followed you for a long time. Longer than you realise."

Billy narrowed his eyes. "What?"

"We have eyes everywhere, Billy. That's what you don't realise.

We've seen the struggles you've been through. We saw the struggles you went through as a child. The resilience you showed to break away. We tried to bargain with your masters for you to join us, but you escaped. And you've slipped our grip for many, many years."

Billy shook his head. "How... How long have you—"

"We've been here in the shadows for a long time. Waiting. Waiting for the perfect moment to rise up. Building an army suitable of taking Britain. And working with our collaborators overseas. To create a new world. A truly united world."

World.

Shit. Billy had no idea about the rest of the world. Nobody did. How could they? There was no way of getting in contact with anyone overseas. Anyone who *did* try to sail across to France never came back.

"What... What's the rest of the world like?"

"You'll find out," The General said. "All of your questions will be answered. On one condition."

Billy had a feeling he knew what was coming. "What condition?"

The General smiled. "We've followed you a long time, Billy. And we've seen how strong you are. We've seen the potential you have. So you join us. You stand with us. Together with us. Or you, your girl, and your dog die, right here, right now."

CHAPTER FORTY-NINE

Billy listened to the General harking on about joining him, and as much as he knew it was an absolutely fucking ridiculous suggestion that he was never going to agree to, he still couldn't see any other way out right now.

The General stood there. Pistol to Faye's head. The rest of his troops behind him, looking on with stony faces. Behind Billy, there were more of them. To the left, to the right, so many of them. Surrounded. Totally surrounded.

He didn't see any way out as he held on to Sophie's hand. As Rex stood by his side. As he looked into Faye's eyes, then the General's eyes.

"You join us," the General said. "You join our training program. You put that strength of yours to good use rather than wasting it in this nothingness you've been living for the last God knows how long. Because we know how strong you are. We've seen how strong you are over the years. We put Sophie here into... into a good life. We give her the best life we possibly can. Same to your dog, too. Old pup looks like he could do with a break. Or... well. Face up to the alternative. It doesn't end well for you. For any of you."

Billy shook his head. He couldn't agree to this guy's demands. He couldn't agree to any of his orders.

And yet...

What else could he do?

He couldn't let Sophie die.

He couldn't let Rex die.

He had to survive so he could fight for his people...

For *everyone*.

He looked around at the Liberators, and it suddenly hit. Looking at them with their glazed eyes. Seeing them all staring back at him.

And then seeing Tristan.

Seeing Tristan, so battered, so bruised.

So broken.

It suddenly struck Billy that they were people too.

That in demonising them for their actions and crimes... they were just people who had been sold a dream.

Sold a lie.

But underneath, right underneath, there could be something else there.

There could be optimism there.

There could be hope there.

He looked around at the people behind him. He looked into these eyes. And he saw how wide they were. He saw how traumatised they were.

He saw the pain they'd seen. How they'd done so many awful, horrible things. How they'd done so many awful things in the name of this man that they barely even looked *present* anymore.

He saw them, and as much as he hated them, as much as he despised them... they were his people.

Because they were people.

And wasn't that the unity he wanted all along?

Didn't he and the General want the same thing, just in horribly different ways?

"A decision," the General said. "You can stick to your precious morals, and you can die. You can prove every hunch I've had about you all these years wrong, and you can die. All of you can die. Or you can join us. You can be united with us. With all of us."

Billy looked into the General's eyes. He tightened his grip around Sophie's hand and looked down at her. Smiled.

"We'll be okay," Billy said. "I promised we'd be okay. Remember?"

She looked up at him like she was confused. Like she didn't understand what was happening or what was going to happen.

And then Billy looked over at Rex.

He felt himself welling up.

Felt his throat tightening up.

Saw Rex staring up at him, wagging that docked tail.

"You're a good lad," Billy said. "You've always been a good lad."

Rex wagged his tail even more. Tongue dangling out of his mouth like a big chunk of ham.

The General cleared his throat.

"As lovely and sentimental as this is... we really do need a decision."

Billy looked around at the Liberators. Looked into all their eyes, one by one.

"Is this what you want?" Billy said. "Is this what you really want? Is this the unity you want? All of you?"

They stared at him. Unmoving. Unflinching.

The General looked at him with a smirk to his face. With a confidence—an arrogance—that showed that he knew just how loyal his people were.

"Of course you do," Billy said. "You've murdered so many people you don't see any way you can possibly turn back now. If it keeps you awake at night, then so be it. But I'll tell you one thing. I'll tell you one fucking thing."

Billy got down on his knees.

He crouched there, right in front of the General.

"I will never join your people. Ever. I will never serve this monster. I will never, ever sell my soul to the fucking devil like you have. Like *you* have."

He looked at Faye when he said those last words. Right at her.

Because he was done with pity.

He was done with longing for the past.

She'd made her fucking choice.

It was on her.

He crouched there on his knees. It was so silent he could hear a pin drop. Birds singing. Crows cawing.

And his heart racing, banging in his skull.

He looked right up at the General. Right into his eyes through tear-drenched eyes. "So do whatever you've got to do. Do whatever the hell you've got to do."

The General narrowed his eyes. His smile dropped, just for a second. And then he shook his head. "That's a shame. A shame you'd see a child die because of your choices."

"I'm with him."

He felt Sophie move to his side then.

Felt her crouch on the ground, right next to him.

Saw her crying.

Saw her shaking.

But saw her staring up at this man—this monster—so confidently.

So defiantly.

"I don't want to die," Sophie said, snot trickling from her nostrils. "But I'd rather die than join your people."

The General's eyes widened. For the first time since meeting him, he looked genuinely stunned. "Wow," he said, puffing his lips out. "Brave. Very brave. What a shame you've made this choice. You would've been an asset. Both of you would've been assets."

He turned the pistol, then.

Pointed it right at Sophie.

Not Billy, but Sophie.

And then he looked right into Billy's eyes.

"Any last words?"

Billy sat there.

Sat there in the silence.

Sat there holding his breath.

Sat there waiting for that gunshot to ripple through the air.

He held Sophie's hand so, so tightly.

"It'll be okay, Sophie. Just—just like I promised. It'll be okay."

His heart raced.

Fear filled his body.

But deep down, he knew he was doing the right thing.

The *only* thing.

He was fighting for his people.

He'd fought for his people.

Right to the bitter end.

"You'll go to hell for this," Billy said. "And one day... one day you'll wake up, and you'll be haunted by this. All of you will be haunted by this."

The General tilted his head. Narrowed his eyes again. His smile widened, just for a second.

And then he nodded. "So be it," he said.

He pulled the trigger.

Billy heard a bang.

And he knew it was over.

CHAPTER FIFTY

illy heard the bang, and he felt his body sinking into the ground.

Because he knew what that gunshot meant.

He knew where the General was aiming.

He knew exactly where he was firing at.

He held on to Sophie's warm hand. Kept his eyes closed.

"I'm here for you, baby," he whispered, crying. "I'm here for you. I won't let go. I won't..."

And then he felt something.

She squeezed his hand back.

"Billy!"

He opened his eyes.

Looked around.

Because she didn't sound distressed.

She didn't sound in pain.

She sounded...

Alive.

He looked around and saw her staring back at him with wide eyes.

Staring at something ahead of her.

First, the shock. The delight like a punch to the gut.

And then the realisation that something wasn't right here.

That something wasn't right at all.

But Rex was still standing. Rex was still alive.

So what was it?

What was happening?

He looked around, and he saw the General standing there.

Blood trickling down from a hole in the front of his head.

The side of his skull was cracked open, and his brain was on show.

And by his side, he saw something that filled him with a shocking realisation.

Faye.

Faye was holding a pistol.

She was pointing it at the General, who slumped over, blood spurting out from his skull.

She looked Billy right in the eyes as chaos and pandemonium kicked up behind the General.

Stared at him with pained, haunted, tearful eyes.

"Go," she said.

Billy didn't need telling twice.

He grabbed Sophie, wrapped his arms around her, stood up, and he fired.

Fired at the three Liberators behind him.

Gunned them all down and watched them fall to the ground, blood splattering out of their chests.

And then he ran.

Ran with Sophie.

Ran with Rex.

Ran as gunshots rang out behind him.

As bullets flew past so close to his head they almost hit him.

He ran to the corner of the house and went to take a right when he saw two more Liberators down there.

He lifted his rifle.

Pointed.

Pulled the trigger.

Nothing came out.

"Shit," he said.

The Liberators ran towards him. Over his shoulder, he saw them fighting each other. Shooting each other. Chaos. Chaos that he'd caused. Chaos that the death of their dear leader had caused.

He saw Faye kneeling there.

Eyes closed.

He saw a Liberator standing over her.

Then pulling the trigger.

And then he looked away.

"Come on," he said. "We've... we've got to run."

He held Sophie's hand, and he ran down the backs of the houses, from garden to garden.

Bullets whizzed over his shoulder.

Shouting and gunshots rang out as they pursued him.

He held Sophie's hand even tighter as Rex ran along like this was all a game, and he kept going.

"We're gonna do this," he said. "We're... we're gonna do this."

He saw a gate up ahead. Nobody out there that he could see. If they could get out of there, they could go into one of the nearby houses. Hide. Or even disappear into one of the fields. Hide in there. Run. Keep running. Never stopping.

He ran further and further towards that gate when suddenly he felt something.

Pain.

Hot pain in the back of his right shoulder.

He flew forward.

Hit the ground, face first.

Bit his tongue and tasted hot, metallic blood.

He lay there, head throbbing. The agony in his shoulder growing stronger. More painful than anything he'd ever experienced. What was happening? What was...

And then he looked up at Sophie.

Saw her staring down at him. Wide-eyed.

"Billy," she said. "They—they shot you. They shot you."

Billy lay there on the ground, and he felt his stomach sink. Because as behind him, the Liberators got closer, he knew what was happening to him now. He knew this was how it ended. He knew he had no other options. He knew his role was fulfilled.

Just like Steve had sacrificed himself for him... it was his turn to make the ultimate sacrifice.

"Sophie, you need to—you need to go," Billy said.

Sophie shook her head. "I'm not leaving you."

She reached down. Tried to drag him. But she couldn't move him at all. And her efforts just cause him pain. Serious pain.

She backed off. Liberators getting closer. Tears rolling down her face. "I won't leave you."

"Listen to me, Sophie—"

"I won't leave you! I—I want to fight for you. Like you fought for—for us."

Billy looked up into her eyes, and as a tear rolled down his face, he smiled. "You can fight for me by running and taking Rex with you. You can fight for yourself by running and taking Rex with you. That's how you fight for our people. You *are* our people now."

She looked down at him with bloodshot eyes. Tears drenching her cheeks. Shaking her head. "I don't... I can't..."

"You can, Sophie. You can. Never, ever tell yourself you can't do anything. Never listen to that voice in your head. Because it's wrong. It's a lie. But now... now you need to go. There's not much time. You need to go."

Sophie stood there and stared at Billy as those Liberators got closer. As they closed in. As their footsteps hammered nearer and nearer.

And she shook her head, and she cried. "Thank you," she said.

"No," Billy said. "Thank *you*."

"For what?"

Billy swallowed a lump in his throat. "For reminding me who I was supposed to be fighting for. Now go."

Sophie shook her head. She wiped her eyes. And then she looked up and then grabbed Rex's collar. "Come on, boy. Come on."

She tried to drag him. But Rex wasn't budging.

He was just staring at Billy.

Tongue dangling.

Tilting his head.

Billy looked at him, and he felt crushed by his confusion.

But he smiled at him.

Because he was going to make it.

He was going to survive.

"You go," Billy said. "Good lad. You go. You... you go with Sophie. Good lad."

Rex tilted his head from side to side.

And then he let out this little yelpy bark. A bark Billy hadn't heard before. A bark that broke him.

But then he jumped towards Billy.

Licked him across the face with that big, slobbery tongue.

And then he ran away with Sophie.

Billy laughed and cried. "Good lad. You'll—you'll be okay. Good lad."

He looked up at Sophie and Rex as they stood at that gate.

Saw her look back at him.

Saw Rex look back at him.

He smiled at them even though pain crippled his gunshot shoulder, weakness filled his body, and salty tears covered his lips.

He smiled at the pair of them.

"Go," he said. "And don't turn back."

Sophie opened her mouth like she was going to say something else.

And then she closed it.

She nodded.

She looked up at the Liberators heading towards Billy.

Looked back at Billy just one final time.

And then she stepped out of the gate, and together with Rex, she disappeared into the unknown.

Billy smiled.

Smiled as he bled out on the ground.

Smiled as the Liberators got closer.

Smiled as he listened to the gunshots and the chaos all around him.

She was okay.

Rex was okay.

They were going to be okay.

He heard the footsteps stop right behind him, and he knew what happened next.

He knew how this ended.

But he was okay now.

He was okay.

He closed his eyes.

Rolled onto his back.

Looked up at the two Liberators standing over him.

"Go on," he said. "Do your worst."

The Liberator on the right lifted his rifle.

Pointed it at Billy.

And this time, there was no escaping it.

This time, there was no running away.

He took a deep breath as the tears rolled down his face, and he smiled.

Because he'd done what he'd had to do.

He'd fought for his people.

He'd protected his people.

And he could do nothing more than that.

"I hope I did you proud, Steve," he said. "I hope... I hope I did you proud, Dad."

CHAPTER FIFTY-ONE

Sophie ran down the street as quickly as she could and didn't look back once.

She kept on running as fast as she could. Her heart was racing. Her chest was tight. She could barely breathe. She didn't want to look over her shoulder. She didn't want to look back. Because she didn't want to see who was coming.

She knew they would chase her. The Liberators weren't going to stop at just Billy. She'd heard the gunshot a few seconds ago. The gunshot when they reached him.

The gunshot when they'd pulled the trigger.

The gunshot when they'd...

No. She didn't want to think about it. She didn't want to say the words.

Killed him.

She thought those words, and she felt empty inside. Totally empty. Totally dead. She felt a traitor. A traitor for walking away. A traitor for running. A traitor for leaving Billy there, all alone.

He didn't deserve to die alone.

He didn't deserve to die at all.

But she'd had no choice.

She'd done what he'd wanted her to do.

As painful as it was… it was what Billy wanted.

She heard Rex panting beside her. Saw him keep on looking back towards where they'd run from. Like he was waiting for Billy to catch up with them. Like this was just a game of hide and seek to him, and any minute now, Billy was going to step out and join them, and everything was going to be okay.

But Sophie knew everything wasn't going to be okay.

She knew things were never going to be okay again.

She ran down the road. Ran through the snow. Ran past the old shops, which were all shuttered up—a life she had only ever known. She heard about the days they used to be open, these shutters. The days these streets used to be busy before she was born. The days when people could walk down a street, any street, and not have to worry about who they might bump into.

A world where people didn't have to worry about anyone or anything.

A dream.

And as she ran right now, as quickly as she could, she knew she wasn't ever going to find any place like that.

She was never going to find a home like that.

But she had to find something.

She had to find somewhere.

It's what she had promised.

It was her job.

It was her duty.

It was her role.

She looked over her shoulder, and she instantly regretted it.

Liberators.

Just a couple of them. Running down the street. Not where she'd come from, but around the corner.

They were holding rifles.

Pointing them towards Sophie as they ran.

And they were running quicker than she could run.

Far, far quicker.

She looked back ahead. Looked up the street. She didn't know how far she'd be able to make it. Those Liberators were going to catch up to her. They were going to be on her in no time at all.

She had to go into one of the buildings. One of the old shops.

She had to hide in there.

She had to pray.

She turned to head into one of the abandoned shops when she saw something else that sent a shiver up her spine.

Two more Liberators.

Running down the street from up ahead.

Right towards her.

She stood there. Heart racing. Body shaking. And she knew she didn't have a choice anymore. They were coming down the street from both directions. She was trapped. She was surrounded.

She had to hide.

She ran over to the shop in front of her. Tried to lift the shutters, but they were solid to the ground. Locked solid.

"Shit."

She ran along. Ran to the next shutter. Tried to lift that.

But again, it was shut.

Locked shut.

She ran to the next shutter, and she grabbed it and tried to lift it, and she felt it.

Felt it rising.

Heard it squeaking as she lifted it, just a little.

She gritted her teeth. Heart racing. "Come on, Rex. You can— you can get inside. You'll be alright in there."

Rex tilted his head. Backed up and let out a little bark. Like he didn't want to. Like he was scared.

"Listen," Sophie said. Fully aware the Liberators were closing in. Fully aware they were approaching from both sides. "It'll be okay. You need to trust me. You'll... you'll be okay in here. I promise you'll be okay in here. Okay?"

He barked again.

Backed up, further away.

And as Sophie crouched here, clinging to the shutter, trying to hold it up with all her strength... she realised she was going to have to go in there herself.

She was going to have to go in there herself if she wanted to survive.

But as she looked at Rex, then at the Liberators, who were so close... Sophie knew she couldn't just leave him.

She wasn't going to leave him to die out here.

She held her breath, and she held on to that shutter, and she saw the Liberators were close to her now.

So, so close to her.

She sat there. Heart racing. Sweat trickling down her face. Tears stinging her eyes.

She looked up at those Liberators, and she held on to Rex.

Held him close.

Ruffled his fur and felt his warmth as she wrapped her arms around his big, furry neck.

"We'll be okay, boy," she said. "I've got you. We'll be okay."

The Liberators ran up to her.

Stood over her, all four of them.

Rifles raised.

Pointed at her.

Pointed at Rex.

She wanted to shut her eyes.

She wanted to close her eyes completely.

She didn't want to see.

But she looked up at the man in the middle, and she didn't shift her eyes from him at all.

She wanted him to stare down at her while he fired.

She wanted him to know what he was responsible for.

She wanted him to remember her gaze when he fell asleep at night.

She wanted to haunt him.

She looked up at him, and she stared into this man's big, blue eyes as she held on to Rex.

"Do it," she said. "Do whatever you have to do. But you'll remember. You'll... you'll remember."

The man's eyes softened.

For just a second, he lowered his rifle.

Like he was seeing through the spell that had been cast over him.

And then he lifted his rifle again and went to pull the trigger.

Gunshots.

Gunshots, right in front of Sophie.

But not from the man.

Not from any of these people.

She watched the blood splatter from the back of the man with the blue eyes.

Watched him tumble to his knees and fall to the ground.

She watched the other three men turn around, try to fire, but all those were sprayed in a storm of bullets, too.

She watched them fall to the ground from where they stood over her as Rex barked beside her.

And behind them, she saw their shooter.

There were two people standing there.

Two men.

Two men she recognised.

One of them was badly beaten. Badly bruised. Barely wearing anything. He looked broken. He looked defeated.

But he was standing.

And he was holding a rifle.

Tristan.

And then, by his side, holding another rifle, Sophie saw someone else.

Her heart picked up.

A warmth fell over her.

For a moment, just a moment, all of her fear melted away, and Sophie felt free.

She looked up at this man's eyes as he stood there, bleeding out of his shoulder where he'd been shot, and a smile stretched across her face.

"Billy," she said.

He staggered over towards her.

Staggered over towards her as she shot to her feet.

As she clambered over the fallen bodies of the Liberators.

"It's okay," he muttered.

"Billy," she said. "Billy."

She landed in his arms.

Wrapped her arms around him as he wrapped his shaky arms around her, and she held him tight.

They both held each other tight.

And for a moment, for just a moment, it didn't matter about the gunshots in the distance. It didn't matter that the Liberators were close by. It didn't even matter that Billy was shot and bleeding badly.

All that mattered was this moment.

All that mattered was that they were here, and they were alive at this moment.

All that mattered was that they were together.

CHAPTER FIFTY-TWO

Billy held on to Sophie as blood pooled out of his shoulder, and for a moment, for just a moment, everything felt okay.

The sound of the gunshots from the Liberators drifted off into the background. The pain and agony in his gunshot shoulder didn't even feel as intense. He could taste blood on his lips, but it wasn't as sickening as it was earlier. He held on to Sophie, and he could've been anywhere. Not in the most perilous moment of his life. Not just yards away from the very people who now wanted to destroy him. Not in grave, grave danger.

But they were together.

Nothing else seemed to matter. Not for that moment.

He felt a nudge on his leg. Looked down and saw Rex staring up at him. And he smiled.

"Hey, lad," he said, crouching down, ruffling the soft fur on his head. "You getting jealous, hmm? You missing out on all the attention?"

Rex wagged his tail, and he licked Billy's face. Slobbery drool went all over Billy's face, which stunk and tasted awful. But honestly, Billy had never been so happy to be attacked by Rex's tongue. He savoured this moment right now.

But then he heard the gunshots behind him. He heard the Liberators' shouts. He knew they'd delivered a shock to them. The General's death at the hands of Faye... that was something Billy was still wrapping his head around.

He couldn't forgive her for what she'd done. For the way she'd contributed to Eastbrook's demise. That sort of shit was unforgivable.

But she'd done the right thing.

In the end, she'd done the right thing.

Made the right choice.

And for that, he had to salute her.

"We should really go."

A voice up to his right. Tristan. His voice sounded raspy like he hadn't spoken much over the last few months. He looked haunted. Beaten and tortured. Like he'd been through a hell of a lot. Unthinkable things.

But he'd helped Billy.

Just when the Liberators closed in on him in the alleyway, just when Billy thought his life was over, he'd appeared out of nowhere, rifle in hand, and he'd taken them out.

He'd helped Billy.

He'd saved Billy.

And now they had to focus on getting away from here.

Together.

Billy stood up. Tears stinging his eyes. His skin felt cold. Every movement hurt. The gunshot wasn't going to be an easy thing to live with. He was bleeding badly, and it wasn't going to get better on its own.

But they didn't have the luxury of getting him any medical attention right now.

Especially not when they were still so close to the Liberators.

Especially when they were nowhere near safe.

He knew he just had to live long enough to get Sophie and Rex as far away from here as possible—as close to safety as possible—and then he'd be happy.

He looked down at her. Saw her standing there and staring at him with a look of sadness. Like the elation of being reunited with him had faded now, and she was beginning to worry about the practicalities of his survival.

He held out his hand to her. Shakily. Felt a little dizzy.

But when she reached out and took his hand, he felt warmth.

He felt peace.

He really felt like everything was going to be okay.

Even if just for a moment, everything was going to be okay.

He looked down at her, tears welling in his eyes. Saw her eyes turning bloodshot, too. Like she realised that this wasn't forever. That he wasn't going to be around forever. Even if he did somehow survive this by some miracle... nothing was permanent. Nothing at all.

And then he thought of Steve.

Dad.

The promise he'd made to him.

The promise to fight for his people.

The promise to fight for everyone.

He took a deep breath of the cold winter air, and he looked around at Rex.

At Tristan.

And then back at the sound of gunshots from the warring Liberators, who he'd tried to reach out to.

Tried to connect with.

He stood there, and he knew he'd fulfilled his promise.

He didn't have to save everyone. That's not what he'd promised.

He'd promised to *fight* for everyone.

And that's exactly what he'd done.

And exactly what he was going to keep doing.

Until the day he died.

Including himself.

He tightened his grip on Sophie's hand.

Looked at Tristan.

Then at Rex.

And then he looked down the road, into the orange sun hiding behind the thick snow clouds.

And as weak as he felt, as much agony as he was in, and as sure as he was that he wouldn't be able to walk very far in the state he was in... he took a deep breath, and he smiled.

"Let's go," he said.

And then they walked.

Walked towards whatever future lay ahead of them.

Surviving the Darkness.

CHAPTER FIFTY-THREE

ive Years Later...

SOPHIE RAN AS QUICKLY as she could through the woods and really hoped she wasn't too late.

It was a stiflingly hot day. The summers always seemed to be getting hotter nowadays. Hotter and hotter every year. Unless the winters were just getting colder, and it felt like summer was even warmer in contrast. She didn't know. Didn't have a clue.

She ran through the woods. Past the trees. Panting. Her feet were sore, and her chest was tight. Butterflies filled her stomach. Nerves crippled her.

All because of the sound.

She'd heard the horn moments ago, and it made the hairs on her arms stand right on end. The hairs on the back of her neck stood tall. She knew what that horn meant. It could only mean one thing. It only ever meant one thing.

A warning.

An alert.

She ran, and the first thought in her mind was: Liberators. Because they were still out there. Of course they were. Sure, they'd set them back a little while when they'd killed the General. Caused a bit of a setback to them.

But with a group as big and powerful as them, a setback wasn't enough to destroy them.

They had to learn to co-exist with them.

They had to learn to hide from them.

They had to learn not to live the way they lived—to live in their world.

It wasn't easy. There was a two-tier society now. The Liberators, who controlled the cities and the towns with their dystopian paradise.

And then people like Sophie.

Survivors.

People who chose not to conform.

And she wasn't judging the people who *did* conform. The kids born into the new world. A lot of them didn't know any other way of life. The Liberators provided comforts. They provided peace. She wasn't going to judge anyone for joining them. It seemed a far more attractive option, after all.

But Sophie was never going to be a part of that.

It might be the Liberators' world now. But Sophie had seen the world change enough in her short life to know that nothing lasted forever. Someone stronger would come along and replace them. Hopefully, someone better.

But there wasn't much point waiting around anymore. There wasn't much point chasing dreams.

She only had one chance at life.

And she had to savour it.

Every moment of survival was a blessing.

She ran until she reached the thicker trees in the middle of the woods, and then she saw it up ahead.

Her cabin.

The old cabin right in the middle of the woods.

She looked up at the wires across the trees. The traps they'd laid. She knew where every one of them was because she'd laid them.

She walked over them. Walking towards the cabin. Knowing full well none of those traps had been tripped.

So it could only mean one thing.

She reached the cabin and pushed open the door, and she saw him sitting there, right in the middle of the lounge.

Tristan. Smiling widely.

On the carpet in front of him, Bella.

The black Labrador who'd become a part of their family two years ago.

Who they'd found roaming the streets and who had taken a particular liking to Rex.

Rex's girlfriend.

Sophie looked across the room and saw Rex sitting there, wagging his tail. He was still alive. Somehow, the old mutt was still alive. Grey. Blind. Deaf. And couldn't move a muscle.

But the bloody dark horse had gone and got another dog pregnant, hadn't he?

Sophie walked across the dark wood of the cabin floor over to Bella, and she saw the little puppies feeding on her.

There were two of them. Just two.

And as she looked down at their perfect, silky little black bodies, she smiled.

Felt warm inside.

"When did it happen?" Sophie asked.

"Just now," Tristan said.

"And where is he?"

"Here," a voice said.

Sophie looked around and saw Billy standing there in the doorway.

He was grey. Thinner than he used to be. Big grey beard now. Looked older than his years.

But he always had this smile on his face.

This quiet confidence.

A look that made her feel comfortable and confident, always.

"Where the hell have you been?" Sophie asked.

"Trying to find you. Has she... Oh, bless. Look at 'em."

Sophie looked back around at the two pups feeding on their mother, and she felt the beauty of them. They reminded her that in a dark world, a world without power, and a world where horrible things happened every single day... there was still hope.

There was still goodness.

There was still joy.

Happiness.

She lifted one of the little puppies. Felt its soft fur in her hands and felt herself melt inside a little bit.

"They got their mother's looks, I see," Billy said.

"Don't let him hear you say that," Sophie said.

Billy walked over to Rex, ruffled his fur. "I can say what I want around this deaf dog, can't I, lad? Can't I?"

Rex just wagged his tail, licked Billy's face, barely even lifting his head.

Sophie stroked Bella. And she stroked these little pups, too. And it felt like, at this moment, everything was good. Everything was okay.

Because they had tough moments. They had horrible moments. Hard times. Times that made her question whether it was all worth it. Times that made her wonder whether it was even worth keeping on going.

But it was the moments like this that made her realise that it was worth it.

That life was worth it. Always.

And that it was worth fighting for.

Sophie looked down at the two pups.

She looked down at their mother lying there, wagging her tail.

She looked over at Rex, who looked on, tired, exhausted, not many nights left in his life, but happy. Content.

And she felt Tristan and Billy's presence, right beside her.

Life as a survivor was tough.

Life as a survivor was always going to be tough.

They were always going to be hiding. They were always going to be fighting. They were always going to be running. And loss was never too far away. Loss was always around the corner. Loss was always close.

But moments like this made it worth it.

Moments like this made everything worth it.

"So. What're you gonna call 'em?" Billy asked.

Sophie looked down at the little girl, and right away, one name came to mind. Only one name she could possibly give. "The girl... the girl's Aoife," she said.

She looked up at Billy.

Saw his eyes clouding a little with tears.

He smiled at her. Nodded. Wiped his eyes. "And what about the boy?"

She looked at the cheeky little boy wagging his tiny little tail, and she smiled.

"I don't know where it came from," Sophie said. "And I don't know what you'll think. But... but I'm going to call him Max."

Billy smiled. Patted her back. "I think Max sounds perfect."

She looked down at Aoife.

Looked down at Max.

Looked at these little bundles of joy and hope, and she smiled.

"Hello, Aoife and Max," she said. "What's your story going to be?"

* * *

THE END

If you want to be notified when Ryan Casey's next novel is released—and receive an exclusive post apocalyptic novel totally free—sign up for the author newsletter: ryancaseybooks.com/fanclub

If you enjoyed this book, check out Outbreak, a gripping post-apocalyptic story from Ryan Casey.